THE FORSAKEN FEW

Cortland Betts

authorHOUSE®

AuthorHouse™
1663 Liberty Drive
Bloomington, IN 47403
www.authorhouse.com
Phone: 1-800-839-8640

First published by AuthorHouse 4/29/2011

ISBN: 978-1-4567-6066-3 (e)
ISBN: 978-1-4567-6067-0 (sc)

Library of Congress Control Number: 2011906809

Printed in the United States of America

*Any people depicted in stock imagery provided by Thinkstock are models,
and such images are being used for illustrative purposes only.
Certain stock imagery © Thinkstock.*

This book is printed on acid-free paper.

IMPRINTING SOULS

ANOTHER START

I WATCHED THE ROAD VERY LITTLE AS I drove down the country-side road back to one of my many old homes. The land had changed greatly since the last time I was here. It had become a modern southern town, one in which a few old traditions were sure to have survived. I still saw a few rebel flags hanging in the back yards which I thought was kinda ironic with the whole "the south will rise again" thing going. The south was permanently part of the United States and nothing any of these red-necks with southern pride could change that. I finally made it into town were the shops were still in the families they had been over two hundred years ago. It was quite a surprise to be honest. I never thought old man Slade would manage to keep his store for more than a year let alone pass it on to his son. I passed the school, where I would start work as the new writing teacher this Tuesday. I weaved my way back out of town and up the side of the town's very own Mt. Gad. I drove about four miles up the mountain before turning into a large driveway that lead to a manor just outside of veiw. This was and had always been one of my homes. It was my third I believe, cannot be sure really, I have been alive for over fifteen hundred years. I, though old as I am, still seem to be one of the youngest of the forsaken that are scattered across the world. Lilith and Cain, on the other hand, are the two oldest of our kind. Cain is a member of our council and Lilith, well, let's say she likes getting into trouble.

I pulled up to the front stairs to find a short older man rushing out to greet me. It was Bryan, my butler. He had been with me since he had black hair and smooth skin. Now he had grey hair and whinkles. His beautiful blue eyes and lean form never faded though. He quickly openned my door and bowed his head, something I was never able to get him to stop doing. He walked just infront of me as we headed up the stairs to the manor.

"I'm glad you finally arrived. The house is magnificient just as you told me it would be. All the arrangements for your stay have been made and I feel you will be quite satisfied with the outcome," Bryan informed me.

"I trust you are right for you have never let me down to this day and you have worked for me for many years. Bryan, I trust your judgement as if it were my own. Just please tell me you got all of the Confederate antiques out of the house," I releaved him.

"Each and every, Sir. Would you like a tour of the house or are you quite satisfied with your memory of it?" Bryan offered.

"Bryan, I may be hundred of years older than you, but my memory is never fading. After all, eternity isn't a punishment when I can simply forget what I did to earn this curse of mine," I reassured him.

I patted Bryan on his shoulder then ran up the stairs to my room. True I could have been in my room in a flash, but I am an old-fashin kind of guy. I prefer to walk and run as a human does. You see the forsaken as we call ourselves are supernatural as the humans would call it. We have been vampires, werewolves, witches, demons, and even bigfoot. We are unnaturally fast, never forget anything, never need to eat or sleep, super strong, and many other super senses and what not. We are simply everything humanity has ever feared except God and Lucifer. Due to the fact that humans have indeed killed several of us and the fact that we like humanity get into wars amongst ourselves, the council has set into place rules to keep us alive and our existance a secret. Thus, if any of us over step our bounds, even by a hair, the council will pass judgment and most likely kill the guilty party.

I took a quick shower and stood on the balcony to dry off in the warm sun. A cool breeze swept past my body as a new presence landed behind me. A tall dark woman stood searching my body with her dark brown eyes. She tossed her jet black hair to the side as her slender leg started to carry her toward me. She put her hand in my own black hair and screwed it up even more, but she always did like things messy. She staired into my blue eyes as her fingers traced the muscles of my chest. She took one step forward and kissed me on the cheek. I shook my head and smiled as I walked into my room to grab some clothes.

"What brings you to my home, Lilith?" I asked.

"Just welcoming you to the neighborhood, Shade," Lilith answered.

"There's more to it than that and we both know it. What do you want?" I demanded.

"Straight to the point. I always liked that about you. I want the council to be destroyed. They have forced us to the brink of destruction with these rules that keep us from being the gods we can be. I'm sick of it. I am like a queen to our people and I'm expected to follow rules that I didn't make my damn self. Cain did catch my interest unlike his bossy father. But he didn't fall too far from the tree," Lilith explained.

"You complain too much. If you want to break rules then don't get caught. Otherwise, get over it. The council is over fifty strong and there are only about two hundred of us left. You would need a great deal of support of which you won't easily find. Is that why you are here? You want my support, don't you?" I questioned.

"Yes. You have pull with over twenty other forsaken all across the world. With your support, they will join us, then we will be half way to victory. You can be my partner, my only partner," Lilith tried.

"Nice try, Lilith, but I'm not interested in you. I'm not interested in a war, just a normal life, well as close to normal as possible. Nothing personal," I answered.

"You're making a mistake, Shade. I will be the queen and then you will bow or die," Lilith warned.

"When you are queen I will acknowledge you as I acknowledge the council now. Till then I'll follow the rules," I informed her.

"If that's the way you want it then it's your mistake," Lilith said in a menicing tone.

"Then so be it. It's time you leave, Lilith. Next time let me know when you're coming. Good-bye," I said bluntly.

Lilith gave me a go to hell look and leapt from my balcony. She landed gracfully on the ground and blurred away. Our speed came in handy when making a quick exit. I turned to find Bryan standing in my door. He bowed his head respectfully. He entered the room and crossed to the balcany enterance.

"Sorry if I was interupting you, sir. I had no idea that you had company," Bryan apologized.

"No you weren't interupting. Did you need something?" I explained.

"Yes. Your new boss, Mr. Kiddle, called and was wondering when you would be preparing your classroom," Bryan explained.

"Could you call him back and tell him I'll be there tommorrow to get ready. Thank you," I requested.

"Certainly, sir. May I ask you to contribute to this very nice charity I saw when I was coming into town?" Bryan replied.

"Yes, two hundred dollars should be quite helpful," I answered.

"It's to build a new library for the school," Bryan informed me.

"Make it three grand. Anything else?" I asked.

"No, thank you sir," Bryan said with a bow which hid a very brilliant smile. You see Bryan is a very kind-hearted man. When he discovered my conditioning, he vowed to save me. He still does not realize that there is nothing he can do to save me, not unless he kills me. He would never even concider it, even to save someone's life. No, Bryan will never be a killer or anything short of a saint.

As Bryan walked away I stretched and decided to see what changes the years had brought to my land. I leapt from the balcony and darted into the woods no more than a blur to any who saw me. The trees had grown quite well for the enviroment they came up in. The small stream that ran to the far east was now more like a small river. In a few years I'll be living next to a river that all the locals try to fish at even though it's private land. I won't be here by then so I won't mind. The vineyards to the north were still kept in exillent condition. They provided me with a valueable source of income. And to the west are the cliffs which I love to sit on and watch the world as it turns so slowly.

This plantation like all the ones I own are paradise to any human and to me they are homes. I own the whole south eastern region as far as the forsaken go. We have territories assigned by the council due to a territorial dispute several hundred years ago. So now the world is divided amongst the forsaken to prevent another war. To the humans however, we are simply the owner of the land on which we live and are no threat to any of them. This is the way most of our kind want it. Everyone is safer that way. Unfortunatly, forsaken such as Lilith believe we should rule mankind as gods. We are being punished enough without tempting fate further.

I took a seat at the highest point of the cliffs and sat there watching the town as the day drew to an end. To me time past by fast as if not at all. Kind of like I blinked and an hour was gone. But to humans, every second counts. They have such a limited time to do everything and

I have all the time in the world. I treasure human life more than my own, but I never confuse the reality of the situation. To humans, I am a monster who must die so they may stay safe. So as every cycle must go, I will kill to protect myself no matter who I must kill.

I sat there for another two hours watching as some humans went to bed early to prepare for the up coming school year, and others simply stayed up just to stay up. The parents sat up talking and discussing while the children slept without a worry in the world. Teenagers stayed up rebeling against their parents and partying the last days of summer away, hoping that it would never end. But as their parents before them, they will discover that everything comes to an end whether we want it to or not. As the last light went out across town, I decided it was time to head back to the house for the remainder of the night. I took one last look at the sleeping town and ran back home.

Bryan like the rest of the town was already in bed fast asleep. I took care not to disturb him as I entered the house. I followed the stairs back up to my bedroom and made a list of things I would need in my classroom. It was not a long list. I would need a laptop to take my work home with me not that I couldn't get in and out of the school as I pleased. I would need lots of pens and pencils to make sure no student goes unable to write as he sees fit. I need a gradebook, a stapler, and most importantly, myself. That should be everything I might need. With that done I had nothing left to do for the rest of the night.

I decided to go out. I knew this great club about forty miles north of here and decided it couldn't hurt to go out tonight. I blurred out of the room, through the door, and down the street. Forty miles would only take me five minutes to cover so I turned around and went back to the house. I changed into a proper clubbing suit and ran right back out the door. The trees swayed as I ran past them. A human at this speed couldn't make out a thing, but I could see everything as if it was right infront of me. My senses are ten times as powerful as a human's making it possible for me to hear and smell someone over twenty miles away. I could see anything within a four mile radius. As for feeling, even the slightest change in air catches my attention. With that said, imagine the wind strong enough to knock the breathe out of you staying agianst your chest. Imagine seeing everything at once without blinking. That isn't even the half of what running as a forsaken feels like.

I got to the club and decided not to wait in line since I was twenty-one as Mr. Hadow. I just blurred past everyone and walked right in. I smiled as I saw the dance floor covered by humans of all shapes and sizes. My smile got even deeper when I realized that several women noticed me the moment I walked through the door. I just walked down to the dance floor so they could come find me if they were brave enough. Well, three were, but I'm hard to please so I let each of them have a dance and had to leave them be. One girl slipped by me and put her number in my pocket with a note that asked me to follow her. I looked at her for a moment, crumpled the note and followed her. She lead me to a private room in the back. She waited for me to walk through the door before shutting and locking it. I smiled a wicked smile which she returned as she danced closer to me. I grabbed her hand and spun her into my arms. We swayed as she slowly turned toward me. Our lips locked and she wrapped herself around me. I smiled and lifted her off her feet. We continued kissing as she got me more enthusiastic I began to change my mind. We tend to get messy when we have sex so it always ends badly for the partner and sex was all this girl wanted. I layed her on the leather couch and smiled as I slid her shirt up and kissed her stomach. She closed her eyes and made a sound of pleasure.

"This won't end well if we persist so I'm ending it now," I whispered in her ear. Before she could even move I was out the door and headed for the exit.

The bouncer spotted me and followed me to the door. As I went out, he stopped and decided to let me go. I smiled and blurred back to the house with and hour left before I could go get anything I needed for my classroom or get breakfast, which I didn't need, but thuroughly enjoy. I stopped and toyed with a mountain lion who thought it was the hunter till I got there. I laughed as I left it in the tree I dragged it up. It jumped down and ran into the night. I turned and finished my run home.

Bryan's alarm was set to go off in an hour so I pushed it back two more. I didn't want him to over-work himself for one who can do as much as I can. I jumped back in the shower to kill the rest of the time before I could go shopping. The shower helped me relax, but woke Bryan up so I had to take him shopping with me. So strange, two men out shopping. What's the world coming to.

We got everything we needed. I treated Bryan to breakfast, which he was very thankful for. Then I sent him home. He insisted on staying to help set my room up, but I told him that it was my job and my responsibility and I planned to keep it that way. He finally gave in and returned home. I made my way toward the school to put my room together when I ran into a short-stocky man at the front door. He looked me over very quickly and smiled.

"Ah, Mr. Hadow. It's a pleasure to finally meet you. I am Mr. Kiddle. I am so proud to finally be able to offer a writing program in our school. I'm sure the students will be very excited to take your class. I hope you enjoy working with us as well. If there is anything you need just ask me and I will do what I can," Mr. Kiddle offered. I shook his stubby little hand and smiled as I noticed my reflection in his bald head.

"I just need to know where to find my classroom," I said honestly.

"Of course. Rose, dear, can you show Mr. Hadow to his classroom," Mr. Kiddle requested.

"Yes, Mr. Kiddle. Hello, Mr. Hadow, how are you? My name is Rose Augusteine," the young lady introduced herself. It was at that moment that I was doomed to die. Just one look at this beyond beautiful young lady and I was hooked. She was magestic. How could such beauty exisit without my knowledge? It doesn't matter for now that I've seen her I can't live without her and I sure can't live with her. It is forbidden for any of our kind to be in love let alone have a steady girlfriend. Damn the predicament I'm in now.

"Are you ok, Mr. Hadow?" Rose asked.

"Yes, I'm fine, just dazed," I answered the goddess before me.

"Dazed by what?" Rose asked.

"A true writer sees beauty in all it's forms," I replied.

"What beauty? I'm the only one here," Rose stated.

"Yes, you are. So which way to the classroom?" I redirected the subject.

"Oh, yes, this way," Rose jumped at the change and hurried down the hall.

I followed Rose half way across the school unable to take my eyes off of her. Each move she made, every step she took, and every brush of her hair had me on the edge of my control. It couldn't be fair to have someone I couldn't stand the idea of staying away from so close, yet still out of my reach. How to be with her without the council finding out? There is no way to know for sure. I have to talk to Cain and accept his advice in this. Maybe he will have a solution for this beauty before me.

"Here we are, Mr. Hadow. I hope you enjoy it here. See ya around," Rose said with a flirty smile that took my breathe away.

"Thank you, Rose," I simply said.

I thought about her all day as I set up my classroom. I believe she thought about me too. I saw her walk by my classroom several times and looked in while trying not to get caught. I smiled slyly to myself as I worked. When I was finished setting up my room, I quickly made my way out of the classroom and down the hall to leave. Suddenly, I ran into Rose and what looked to be her family. She blushed as she realized who I was. I smiled and examined her family.

"Mom, dad, this is Mr. Hadow. He's the writing teacher," Rose introduced.

"It's a pleasure to meet you. It looks like your son's a writer or he keeps a journal," I greeted.

"Yes he is. How did you know that? He only just registered," Mrs. Augesteine asked.

"He's carrying a notebook with a pen tucked in the spiral. A sure fire sign that he enjoys writing in certain quiet places," I pointed out.

"You're right but that doesn't mean you're going to be a good writer," Rose's little brother prompted.

"It tis a cold night on a midwinter's day along the traveler's way. Even in the darkness of the night the traveler kept along his way. As the wind began to stir and howl, the traveler stayed his course without hesitation. He never turned nor stayed nor let anything in his way as he traveled his way. And as the night hit its darkest the traveler pulled down his hood to reveal an old dying man who at that moment fell dead on Deadman's Way," I told.

"Wow, that was actually kind of cool. I think I might like your class if that's what you're going to teach me," Rose's brother said with a grin.

"I will teach you to listen to yourself, and you will do the rest," I told him.

"I'm sure you'll learn plenty from Mr. Hadow," Mr. Augesteine added.

"Thank you for your vote of confidence, Mr. Augesteine," I said.

"Tim has some talent I must admit. Perhaps you'll help him find his true calling," Mr. Augesteine joked.

"That's what I'm here to do. Well, I have a meeting I have to go to so I'll let you guys get back to your day. It was a pleasure meeting all of you," I said as I kept glancing at Rose. She just stood there staring at me, her cheeks blood red and her smile weak and hopeful. I smiled at her and walked away as best I could for I knew this may be the last time I see her after I get done talking to Cain.

I got out of the school and blurred out of sight, on my way to the council room, where Cain basicly lived.

THE COMPROMISE

THE COUNCIL CHAMBER WAS JUST AS IT was over four hundred years ago when Cain asked me to join the council as a member. Fifty doors lined the walls like picture frames waiting to recieve their pictures. I turned to the highest door just before it opened. A man no older than seventeen stood in the opening. His sandy-blonde hair sank down over his turquoise eyes. His muscled build was nullified by his small size. He looked down at me with a gaze that made most men srink in fear. His expression lightened when he realized it was me. We can sense each other's presense but cannot tell who the forsaken we sense is.

"Hello, old friend," Cain greeted me.

"It's good to see you. How are things going with the council?" I asked to make light conversation.

"It's getting interesting. I've been hearing rumors of an uprising among our own. A power struggle just over the horizen. What have you heard of this struggle?" Cain presented.

"Lilith approached me. I told her I was neutral as always and that my contacts were not hers. I come about different matters. Matters by which I need your council," I answered.

"What troubles you?" Cain asked tentively.

"You know of the problem we've had about forsaken falling in love. I told you it was a decision that could be made. I was wrong," I informed him.

"Wrong about what?" Cain asked in a menacing tone.

"When it happens, there is little choice to be made. One can simply keep his head straight," I explained.

"How do you know of this?" Cain inquired further.

"It has happened to me. I came here to you as soon as I could to seek your advice about this matter," I finished.

"This is a grave matter. How well can you control your impulses?" Cain questioned.

"Better than I thought I would at first sight. It's getting easier the more I see her. She's compelled toward me as well. What shou I do?" I wished to know.

"Join the council," Cain almost ordered.

"Excuess me?" I asked in amazmnt.

"Join the council and while we figure out how to resolve this I will protect you," Cain offered.

"And what of the girl?" I inquired.

"I vow that no harm will befall her. Shade, you have been my friend for centuries. I know you to be wiser than most of our kind. I trust your judgement. Now do you accept my offer?" Cain explained.

"Yes, Cain, I will join. Is there anything else we need to discuss while I'm here?" I decided.

"I just need you to be careful and see where this takes you," Cain answered.

"I will. You have almost nothing to worry about," I said.

Cain laughed as I walked away. He shut the door and I blurred away, back to my current home to face my new reality. It took me about two hours to make the trip so when I got back to the manor Bryan was standing at the door waiting for me. He smiled as I came into focus and moved to greet me. I smiled back and blurred to the top of the stairs. He gave me a funny look. I just smiled and shook my head.

"Is something wrong, sir?" Bryan asked with a sense of alarm.

"Only if falling in love is a problem," I retorted as I walked past him.

"But isn't it for a forsaken?" Bryan puzzled. I began climbing the stairs.

"Only if it blinds us," I called back to him.

"Sir, should I be ready to move at any time then?" Bryan asked.

"No Bryan, we're safe," I yelled from my room.

I looked at the calender. I had three days before school started.This left me little time to prepare for what most certainly laid before me. I did not know the full extent of what I would have to endure to be with Rose, but I knew that we would have to wait until after she graduated. I went to my safe and got out four hundred dollars. I smacked my hand with it several times as I decided where to go shopping for more clothes. I decided to go looking through Mississippi. It was one state over and I had not been there in around a hundred years. I wen t down stairs to tell Bryan what I was doing, but found him making lunch so I left a note and blurred out the door.

I found a nice clothing store after about two hours of running around Mississippi. It had a wonderful supply of collared shirts and dress pants. I got about ten different colored shirts and just as many black dress pants before deciding that I had enough to get me started.The cashier had been watching me make my way around the store and smiled with great joy as I approached the counter to check out.

"How are you today, sir?" the cashier asked.

"I'm great thank you, and yourself?" I returned.

"Better now. So are you from around here?" she asked as she began scanning the clothes I had picked out.

"No, I'm just here getting clothes," I answered.

"That's a drag. You look totally hot and I was hoping to talk you into asking me out," she informed me.

"Well thank you. You look very good yourself, but I'm from out of state. Why don't you try this man coming in right now?" I insisted. The man I implied was around twenty with a toned body that would complement her slender form rather nicely. The cashier bit her lip and smiled.

As I moved toward the door I heard her ask the man if he needed any help. I could tell by his reply that I had just helped the girl out. I slid out of sight before I blurred away. I barely got through the door before it closed but other than that it was smooth sailing all the way home.

I got hime to find Bryan on the couch watching tv, a very rare occurence. I blurred up to my room and put all my new clothes up while taking off all the tags. When each article of clothing was hanging up I picked up all of the trash and took it downstairs to the garbage which I then emptied. Unfortunatly, as I walked back into the house, I walked right into Bryan who was getting a snack.

"Very sorry, sir. I didn't hear you come in," Bryan apologized.

"It's quite alright, Bryan. I didn't want to disturb you. You so rarely watch television anymore that I believe you should do it more often, or at least not get interupted when you are watching it," I declared.

"Thank you, sir. How was the shopping trip?" Bryan asked.

"It was refreshing. I haven't been to Mississippi in a while so it seemed like a good idea," I told him.

"Very good, sir. Another forsaken came by," Bryan said.

"Who and what did it want?" I inquired.

"His name was Phillip. He brought you a package. I believe he left it on your bed," Bryan explained.

"Thank you, Bryan," I said as I ran up the stairs to find out the nature of the visit.

When I got in my room, I spotted the red box that I didn't notice when I was putting up my clothes. It didn't stand out on my red comforter so I understood why I had over looked it, but what could it be? I slowly walked over to my bed and sat down next to the box. I picked it up and listened for just a moment before deciding it wasnt a bomb sent by Lilith. I quickly ripped the bow in half to see what was inside. It was a cell phone. No sooner had I openned it when it started ringing. The screen said it was Cain calling, so I answered.

"Hello," I answered.

("I've got great timing don't I?") Cain asked over the phone.

"Yes, you do. What's the phone for?" I wondered aloud.

("To keep in touch. You're a member of the council now and we have to be able to get in touch at a moments notice, so I sent you a phone. And yes I remember how much you detest phones, but it's the only way,") Cain explained.

"I understand. Is there something important I need to know?" I inquired.

("Yes. Our next council meeting is Tuesday at seven that night. Is there a problem with that?") Cain informed.

"No I'll be done at the school by five so I can be there in no time," I answered to the fullest.

("Exellent! I'll see you then,") Cain said before he hung up.

I looked at the phone for a minute then grabbed the instruction manual so I knew what I was doing with this blasted thing. It only took me a few minutes to read. I found the charger and just plugged it into the wall next to my bed. I stuck the phone in my pocket and went downstairs to join Bryan on the couch for what ever show it was that got his attention. It was some old-timey show that I just could not get into. So I went up the mountain to explore. I pushed up the mountain through the tree lines until the sun was hot on my face. It brought back an old memory that took place across the Atlantic Ocean.

It was around the time where vampires were a big epidemic in Europe. Of course, it was the forsaken who developed a taste for blood that started the whole thing. We had a few who pretended to do what we did, but they never had any real strength or power. We forsaken, however, did. I hunted in a small town to promote a detective game for myself. I wanted them to find me, to try and kill me. After months of me killing once a night, they finally came to me and pointed the finger. This prompted a challenge for me to prove I was smarter than them so I told them to tie me up on a cross and wait for the sun to come up. I told them if I was the vampire, I would surely die. Then I declared that if I did not burn in the sun that they were to release me and that I would leave forever. They fell for it. As the sun came up I smiled and made an illusion of fire engulfing me. While the illusion kept the villagers interested, I made my way out of the village with the sun on my face the whole time. No one saw me leave, just an illusion of a man burning for being a demon of the night.

I sat at the mountains rounded peak and remembered some of the things I had done. I remembered everything even the very deed that had forsaken me. To be forsaken is to commit such a crime that man cannot punish you enough to satisfy God. And so he punishes you with an eternity of remembering what you have done, and living with it each and every day. Lilith simply defied God, while Cain killed his own brother. The now dead Judas betrayed Jesus. There are countless other forsaken sins but there has not been a new forsaken in over a thousand years. Now all sins happen every day. Sin has become so comon that had Cain been born in this day he would never have been forsaken to begin with. I, on the other hand, would be forsaken no matter what year I was born or how bad sinning got. My sin is unforgivable, even to me.

I got restless so I decided to go back to the house and see if that stupid show was over. I dodged through the trees on my way back down, making a sport of it to help ease my mind. I launched myself onto my balcony and came sliding to a halt as I heard a familar voice down stairs. What could she be doing here? I decided to go down and find out.

As I slowly decended the stairs the voices implied that they were in the living room watching tv. Of course, Bryan must have told her I had gone up the mountain. I blurred back up the stairs and jumped down from my balcony landing twenty feet from the back door. I tried to calm myself as a walked toward the door. I had never been in this situation before and had no idea how I was going to handle it. I walked through the back door and made my way through the clean white kitchen and turned just as I passed the stairs to see her beautiful face look up at me, filling with excitment as she realized it was me. Bryan stood up and took a bow.

"This is Rose Augesteine here to see you, sir," Bryan introduced.

"We've met," that was all I managed to say.

Rose blushed as she took a few steps toward me and held out her hand. Without thinking I took her hand and kissed it. She giggled with delight as I blushed this time. Bryan smiled now fully y understanding what I had said earlier. He inclined his head toward me and excused himself. Rose and I watched nervously as he passed by us. As soon as he was out of sight, Rose took a step forward, wrapped her arms around my neck, and kissed me. I couldn't help but to kiss her back, but this was different than any other time I had kissed a girl since I had been forsaken. There was no power in it, just passion, like I couldn't hurt her if I tried. She pulled away from me and her smile widened, but without warning she fainted.

"Bryan!" I exclaimed.

Bryan came running out of the kitchen and knelt down next to her. I picked her up and laid her on the couch. Bryan slid over so he was right next to her again. I gave him an apologetic look, which he ignored. Bryan checked her pulse then relaxed a bit. He looked up at me and smiled.

"She's fine. What ever you did to her made her heart rate soar, so she fainted. She'll be just fine. So she's the one you fell in love with?" Bryan confirmed.

"From the first moment I saw her," I replied without hesitation.

"And what of the council?" Bryan inquired.

"They've been taken care of," I answered.

"I'm happy for you, sir. I believe this is a sign that you're on the road to redemption. This is your compromise for a chance at a new life. I'm glad I'm here to witness this," Bryan said with tears of joy running down his face.

"We will see, won't we?" I replied unsure of how to take what he said.

"We need to get her home," Bryan said while trying to choke back the sobs.

"Did she drive?" I asked.

"No. A friend dropped her off," Bryan answered.

"I'll take her home then," I offered.

"No, sir. I'll take her home. I've already made up a story to keep her out of trouble. If you don't mind helping me get her to the car, she should be awake by the time I get her home," Bryan suggested.

"Ok," I agreed.

I picked Rose up and carried her to the car while Bryan went to get the keys from the kitchen. I strapped her in as Bryan was walking out the door. She murmured something as I fastened her seatbelt. I couldn't quite make it out. Bryan got in the driver's side and started the car. He nodded to me and drove away. I thought about it for a while but couldn't figure out what she she murmured to me in the car.

THE NEW YEAR

B RYAN GOT HOME THAT NIGHT STILL SMILING. It must have gone well, otherwise he wouldn't be quite so happy. I decided to go see how Rose was doing. I'd stay out of sight, of course, but I just had to know she was alright. I blurred through each street trying to find her scnt. It was so strong that when I finally did find the source, I almost ran right to her. I quickly found out which was her room and picked a spot to watch her from. Since her bedroom was in the front of the house, I decided to sit on the roof across the street. I had no problem seeing or hearing what was going on.

Rose walked into her room quickly followed by her mother who looked concerned. What had Bryan told them? Rose sat down on her bed, while her mother began what looked to be a lecture. I wanted to rush over there to make sure she didn't get into any trouble, but I couldn't.

("Rose, what were you thinking. You shouldn't have gone to him to get advice. Your brother's trying to follow in your footsteps, and your father doesn't want that. You running to Mr. Hadow for help on your writing will just give your brother the same idea. Now your father's furious with you and he'll be sure to keep you and your brother away from each other as much as possible now. Can you please just help your father get your brother on the right track?") Mrs. Augusteine lectured.

("Mom, it's his life to live as he wants, and I won't make him do anything. I'm not telling him to do as I do, he's just doing it. Please, mom, if Mr. Hadow can help me with my writing then let him. I couldn't take his class, so he's willing to help me on his own time,") Rose pled.

("No!") Mrs. Augusteine said in a finalized tone.

("You won't be able to stop me for long!") Rose yelled.

At that instant her father walked in. He had the look of a wild man. He pushed his wife to the side and grabbed Rose by her arm. I wanted to just slam into him and rip his arms off so that he could never grab her again. I held my ground for fear that if I showed my true nature, Rose would run and I would die as would she.

("Your mother said no and that is that! Do you understand me little girl? We gave you life and until we're dead you do as we tell you!") Mr. Augusteine exclaimed.

I couldn't take it anymore I blurred to the ground and picked up a rock. I jumped back onto the roof and launched it at her father. The window shattered and Rose's father hit the ground out cold. Rose quickly got over the shock of what had happened and looked out the window as I blurred away.

My only regret for throwing that rock at her father, well two regrets, are that it didn't kill him and that she may now know that I am not human. It scared me that she may now know that I am a monster and decide to never look at me again, but I made a choice and it's too late to change that. I went up to the cliffs to sit and watch the world again. I saw the headlights leaving Rose's house headed toward the hospital and knew that I had done wrong, but couldn't and wouldn't apologize for it. If the council decided to punish me than so be it. I have seen beauty beyond compare and can die a happy thing without any real regrets save one. That I didn't know Rose for all of my life or at least when I was human.

After Rose's parents returned home early that morning I went back to the house. Bryan sat up waiting for me. He fell asleep on the couch with the television on. It's sad how so many choose to rely on me when I feel as though I can't even rely on myself. How can Bryan see any goodness inside me when I feel as though there isn't any? I shook my head as I walked up the stairs deciding to use my bed for a change. I walked in and started taking off my shirt when a voice caught my attention.

"How beautiful your body is. Shade. You are very strange. You don't fall for my charm like almost everyone else does. Why is that?" the voice toyed with her thoughts.

I finished taking my shirt off before turning to meet Lilith's gaze. She was sprawled across my bed wairing an extremly short crimson dress. Was she honestly trying to seduce me again? I threw my shirt into the dirty clothes hamper and leaned against the wall. Lilith blurred up to me and pressed her lips to mine. Yes, I could do more with her than any human I know, but I just wasn't interested in that. I put my hand on the center of her chest and pushed her back a few inches.

"I'm simply not interested in that particular means of fun," I told her.

"Are you a virgin?" Lilith taunted.

"No, Lilith. I'm no virgin. I'm just not that into you, or anyone else for that matter," I retorted.

"Liar," Lilith spat.

"How dare you call me a liar in my own home!" I exclaimed.

"Careful, Shade. Don't want your butler coming to his death. Besides, I can smell her. The council should know all about this my little pet," Lilith threatened.

"They already do. If you insist on challenging me then one day, I'll have to put you down," I warned.

"Ha. You put me down. Never!" Lilith argued.

With that Lilith pushed me into the wall hard enough to put a hole in it. I slammed her arms down and pushed her several feet away. I pushed off the wall and grabbed her throat. Before she got a chance to react, I stepped behind her, grabbed her leg, and threw her out the balcony window. I ran and jumped down after her. As I landed she threw an upper-cut that knocked me off my feet. She took a step forward and grabbed my foot and began spinning me around. She let me go with enough force to bury me ten feet into the mountain side over two hundred yards away from the house. As I slid back through the hole I made she grabbed me by the throat and slammed me into a rock.

"Remember who is stronger," Lilith ordered.

"Only time will tell," I spat.

Lilith screamed at the top of her lungs. The noise that came out of her mouth was pure agony that I'm sure the whole town heard. She rammed her knee into my gut and followed it with a punch to the face. I quick slipped out of concousness.

When I woke up, I was in my own bed with a note on my bedstand. I looked around and tried to see straight, but that was harder than I remembered it being so I just closed my eyes. I heard Bryan's voice flow up the stairs as the sound of footsteps followed.

"Are you ok, sir?" Bryan asked sounding quite concerned.

"I will be," I replied.

"Lilith left the note. It warns you to watch those close to you next time you choose to challenge her," Bryan informed me.

"Sorry, Bryan, but the only way to handle a bully," I began.

"Is to never back down. I know, sir, but I must say that fighting is never the best solution," Bryan finished.

"With Lilith it is," I added.

"I can see that she is very hard headed, but," Bryan started.

"She won't give up till she is dead," came a voice from the door.

Bryan spun around to see who interupted him. I sat up and looked at Cain as he walked into the room. He looked at me for a moment then smiled and turned to Bryan. I started to get out of bed when cain took another step toward me and nodded for Bryan to leave. Bryan turned to me and I nodded that it was ok. Bryan took a small bow and quickly exited the room allowing Cain and I to talk in private.

"She's still so very bold and persistant," Cain recalled.

"That's something that will never change. We both know that. Someone's going to have to kill her before too much longer," I agreed as I stretched.

"We can't touch her unless she comes after the council directly and no, not just after a member," Cain added as he caught the sly look that crossed my face.

"Then I guess we have to sit and wait," I shrugged.

"Unfortunatly, that's right. We have to wait until she makes her move," Cain verified.

"So what brings you out of the council chamber?" I inquired.

"Two things, really. Are you ready for tomorrow's meeting?" Cain asked.

"I've been out for over twenty-four hours?" I blurted.

"Have you forgotten that we get stronger as we get older?" Cain asked with a worried look on his face.

"Strength is nothing to me. And to answer your question, yes, I'll be ready," I informed Cain.

"Good," Cain said with delight.

"What is the other matter that brings you to my home?" I asked.

"Ah yes. I came to meet the girl," Cain answered.

"She is unaware of what I am for now. I don't want to scare her. I want to gauge how she will react. If I gauge her on the bad side, she'll nevr know. Is that fair enough for you?" I explained.

"That will work nicely. If she gauges well, tell me so I can meet her," Cain practicaly ordered.

"Of course," I replied.

Cain smiled and nodded his head in delight. He walked out the door and down the stairs. I followed him to the front door and opened it. He nodded his farewell, which I returned. Then He blurred out the door and out of sight. Bryan walked out of the livingroom with a concerned look on his face, one that troubled me.

"Will you turn Miss. Rose over to him, sir?" Bryan asked.

"He won't risk hurting her for fear of losing my political backing. Don't worry, she's safe," I assured him.

"Thank you, sir," Bryan said with a bow. He went back into the livingroom to continue cleaning.

It's funny how I told him she would be safe when I can't even convince myself that it is true, that she is safe with my love for her. Even though the attraction between us is like magnets, yet stronger for we cannot be pulled apart, I fear she has been put into grave danager. With this running through my head, I made an attempt at getting ready for the day ahead of me. I had school and a meeting within the next thirty hours. How annoying to be put under this much preasure. Only a week ago, I didn't have a care in the world. Now I've got four if you count school.

The next couple of hours passed relatively fast concidering I kept busy and had way too much to worry about. I arrived at the school with high hopes of a good day. It was still only seven so I had an hour before any classes would start, and well, I only had two classes to worry about. The first one was second period and the second was sixth period. That left me with most of the day to relax or worry which was more likely.

Mr. Kiddle knocked on my door at about fifteen till eight. He looked kind of excited, but still very nervous. I smiled and waved for him to come in. He shut the door behind him and kind of wabbled to my desk. He looked over the basicly bare classroom before deciding to talk.

"So are you excited?" Mr. Kiddle asked.

"Yes, I believe I am. You look to be a little nervous. Are you alright?" I inquired.

"I have to make a speech in about an hour, and I've got nothing," Mr. Kiddle explained breifly.

"Do you need some help writing a speech?" I asked with a smile. I loved speeches as long as I wasn't the one giving them.

"If you would be so kind," Mr. Kiddle basicly begged.

"Let's see. Here's a pen and some paper. Write this down. Students and staff of Mt. Gad High, I would like to welcome all of you to an exciting new school year, where as always, anything is possible. Keep in mind that you can find new friends around every corner, and don't be afraid to be bold and do the unimaginable. Let us all try to make this year wonderful, for it will take all of us. Now let's start this year off right and remember to follow the rules, learn what the teachers ask, and most importantly, have fun. How does that sound?" I said off the top of my head.

"It's fantastic. How did you come to be so creative?" Mr. Kiddle admired.

"It's natural. We can't learn to be creative. We simply are," I answered.

"Well, thank you very much, Mr. Hadow. This speech will do wonders. Enjoy your first day," Mr. Kiddle thanked warmly.

I nodded in acceptance as he walked out the door. How did that man get this job, I wonder? Well, it sounds like he'll be cutting into my first class of the day so I need to write down an assignmemt as homework. I got up and went to the board. I picked up the expo marker and tinkered with it for a minute while I came up with an assignment. It came to me as a rather simple asignment that I might enjoy reading. I began writing it on the board:

Due tomorrow at the start of class is a two page story about what it would be like if you lived fifteen hundred years ago. All assignments must be hand-writen.

I smiled to myself as I finished writing it down. I heard a giggle at the door. Rose was standing there watching me. I smiled warmly and waved her in. A slightly shorter girl followed her in. Rose's friend had blonde hair that fell just past her shoulders. She smiled as she followed Rose to the desks. They both took a seat as I put the expo back.

"To what do I owe this visit?" I asked.

"Mary and I are office aids this period. We thought we'd come see how you were doing," Rose answered.

"It looks like you've already run all of them off," Mary laughed.

"Not yet. They probably won't stick around after they see what I've got in store for them," I replied.

"And what's that?" Rose asked in a flirty manner.

"We can keep a secret," Mary added with a quick wicked look at Rose.

"Sorry, but it's not so easy to explain as put to practice," I told them.

"Then teach me," Mary demanded while bitting her lip.

Rose looked at her with shook and then at me. I never took my eyes off Rose, which Mary noticed. Rose suddenly got up and rushed to the door. She turned around and waved for Mary to come on, but Mary wasn't paying attention.

"Mary!" Rose exclaimed.

"What," Mary jumped.

"We're going to be late," Rose said.

"Crap!" Mary yelled just then taking her eyes off of me.

Rose mouthed "sorry" as she pushed Mary out the door. I gave her an understanding nod before the door shut. I turned back to my desk and took a seat. Rose's black shirt had a silver rose on it. It was ironic. Her blue jeans hugged her hips tightly. I sat there and picked apart the image of her until the bell went off. My classroom began slowly filling with teenagers who didn't want to be here but preferred my class to the alternative. Rose's little brother, Tim, walked in just infront of some big kids. One of them pushed him out of the way.

"Settle down," I called.

It took a minute, but they finally all took a seat. However, none of them, except Tim, got quiet. I stood up this time.

"I CALLED FOR QUIET!" I yelled.

That time they all got quiet. Every eye was on me now and that was the way I wanted it. I grabbed my attendance sheet and walked before the class. They all watched as I made all of them move into aphibetical order. Each and everyone of them, including Tim, groaned about the seating arrangement. I put my hand up for them to settle back down and this time they didn't have to be told twice.

"I am Mr. Hadow. This is a writing class. You may sit where you want when you earn that right. Until then you sit where I assigned you. You have an asignment on the board that is due tomorrow. My expectations are simple. Write what you feel. No vulger language or you will be moved out of my class. I need each of you to keep in mind that you are responsible for grammar and spell checks. I will count off for them. My priority, however, is your imagination, which by this age of yours has usually faded. Any questions?" I explained in detail.

No hands went up. I did hear a few chuckles, but I would handle them when it came down to it. The intercom kicked on and called all the students to the gym. I waved my arm for them to go and they all practically ran out of my room.

The next class went slightly smoother, but as I said, I wasn't worried about my classes. I went by the office and thanked Mr. Kiddle for my first day and told him that I would see him the next day. I got in my car and went home. I checked in with Bryan and made sure everything was ok. Then I blurred away to the council chamber for the meeting.

I was about an hour early. Cain and Hon were making preparations. Hon was a big man with black hiar and brown eyes. His skin was very dark like he had spent way too much time out in the sun, which he had. They looked up when I entered the room. I just walked and started helping them with the set up. The council room quickly filled up after that. When everyone was there Cain jumped to his door, as did everyone else. I stood alone on the floor waiting to be told where I would stand from this day forth.

"I call this meeting to order. The first order of business is our newest member. Everyone, please welcome Shade to the council," Cain announced. Several of the council members began clapping to welcome me. The others simply nodded in acceptance. Cain raised his hand calling for silence. "Shade, please take this door across from me. You have in your years earned it."

My eyes widen as I realized that Cain had just made me his equal. I did a backflip into the doorway, where I was looking straight into Cain's eyes. Murmurs broke out all across the council chamber as I took my place above all of them. This time I raised my hand to silence them and it worked. Cain smiled at the results, they may not have liked it, but they accepted me.

"The next order of business, fellow forsaken, is the rumors of an uprising," Cain announced.

"It is true that Lilith plans an uprising to wipe out the council," I added. Cain looked at me and nodded.

"Then what do you propose we do?" an extremely small man called from one of the lowest doors.

"Knome, my friend, we can do mothing," Cain called down to him.

"Then why bring this up?" the tallest of the council inquired.

"To be prepared for the chance that she could get the support she needs. Council members will be her targets. We must be prepared though we cannot take the initiative. We can still be ready and waiting. Do you agree?" I answered.

The council chamber filled with cheers of agreement. Cain once again nodded to me this time his smile was unmistakable. He was happy to have help with this position of his and now I understood why he had been trying for so long, and why he was willing to make that compromise. He held up his hand to silence the now restless council. Silence swept the council chamber once again.

"Then it is settled. At the first sign of an uprising, we will destroy Lilith and all who stand with her," Cain declared.

Each and every member of the council nodded in acknowledgment. It was decided, Lilith would die if she attacked any of the council or the council chamber itself. In truth, I was happy for Lilith would never give up, which meant that she would one day die at our hands, preferably mine.

ALL THE BULLIES

IMADE IT HOME BY THE TIME Bryan was getting ready for bed. He looked at me as I walked through the door. His smile was warm, but there was something he wasn't telling me. I paused and examined him closer. He tried to walk away, but I blurred infront of him.

"What is it?" I demanded.

"Nothing, sir," Bryan tried, but he has always been a terrible liar.

"We both know that is not true," I said without any intention of giving up.

"She was here. She knows," Bryan said weakly.

"Rose knows," I said shocked and scared.

"No, sir. Lilith, she knows where you were. She told me to warn you that you were first to die. I told her I would not and she threatened my family," Bryan explained.

"She will die. I promise you, Bryan. She will not get near your family," I swore.

He nodded weakly and walked past me. I clenched my fist and blurred up the mountain where i ran into a boulder to release some of my anger. The boulder crumbled like Lilith soon would. I pulled out the phone Cain gave me and dialed his number. It rang twice before he answered.

("What's wrong, Shade?") Cain answered.

"She knows I'm on the council. I'm going to be her first target," I told him.

("Damn! You aren't safe right next to her like that,") Cain blurted.

31

"Doesn't matter. Cain,I need you to keep Lilith shut down. If she doesn't have back up,I may be able to take her," I tried.

("Not after what happened the other night,") Cain snapped.

"You put me in the council as an epual to you because you trust my judgement, Cain. If I can't stop her, killing me will give the council the opening they need," I explained my, yes, foolish plan.

("Completely out of the question!") Cain exclaimed.

"Cain! I trust you as you trust me. Just trust me. No one else outside of Lilith will try this. If we get rid of her, we finish any chance of chaos amongst our kind. Cain, let me handle Lilith," I bargined.

("I couldn't stop you if I tried, could I?") Cain asked though he already knew the answer.

"No, you couldn't," I replied.

("Very well, do what you must,") Cain submitted.

I hung up the phone and looked over the town. I knew if I died that Cain would never forgive me, but it was a risk I had to take. I knew there was a great chance that I would die, but I didn't care. This was me protecting Rose, Bryan, Cain, all forsaken, and all of the human race. Lilith would destroy everything so I didn't see any other way. At least I got to meet Rose, to look upon her beauty, to taste her breathe, to feel her smooth skin on my own. Having done those things I can die happy, happier than I thought I'd ever be. I never thought a God would curse me either, but we see how that went.

My eyes darted straight to Rose's house. Her light was the only one on. I wondered why and blurred down there. I leapt onto the roof across from her room to find her studying. She looked as htough she was having some trouble. How I longed to go to her and offer my help so that I may be close enough to touch her. In truth I am only twenty-two years old physically. It's strange to be so old and yet feel so young. I watched her until she decided to turn in. As she turned out the light I blurred back to the cliff to watch the silent town as it slept, unaware of the killer in their midst.

I sat on the cliff for what seemed like a week, but was actually an hour, before I decided to go back to the house. I had only been in town a few days, and I already had more tying me here than anywhere else. It's a strange feeling, at least to me, to be tied to anything. It kind of made me happy. I believe what ever time I've got left will be a time of constant happiness in my very long life, and I welcome it with open arms and a very open heart, at least for the beautiful Rose.

I didn't find much to do beyond thinking as the night went on. I took an early shower and took my time preparing for the day as it was my second day at work. I went online to check my checkings account. Yea, I'm still rich so I'm not worried about any of my dozens of bills. I cooked breakfast and made sure there was some for Bryan. I learned to do alot over my years, and yes, cooking was one of them. It was finally time for work. Bryan's alarm had just started going off as I walked out the door, complements of me, of course.

I got to school early as I intend to all year. I decided to roam the halls between my classes to help pass the time. Judging by my memory of yesterday, which was perfect, I only taught about one-sixth of the students who attended this school. It kind of sucks knowing that so few people like writing. Well, I won't let the none writers spoil what time I've got left. I ran into Mary just outside of my classroom. She followed me in. I tried to start setting up, but she was kind of in the way.

"Can I help you, Mary?" I asked.

"You sure can, if you want to lock the door," Mary answered.

"Why would I lock the door?" I asked to humor her.

"So we won't get caught, silly," Mary replied.

"Caught doing what?" I continued.

"Making out and what ever else we decide to do," Mary answered modestly.

"And why would I risk my job to do that?" I inquired.

"You know I'm hot. I know you're hot. So what's the problem?" Mary wondered.

"I'm a teacher," I answered without looking at her.

"So. You know you want me and Rose," Mary tempted.

"Mary, go to class," I told her.

"Ok, spoil-sport," Mary whined as she turned to leave.

I was releaved when she actually went out the door. I thought she was going to lock it and try to rape me. She was half right, but I don't know what made her think I wanted her. I went back to the board and wrote the next assignment on it. This one was an easy one. They simply had to write about what inspired them. Nothing to it, at least for me or someone without a nervousness problem.

The first bell rang so I decided to take a seat and wait the first period out here in my room. It may have been because I was hoping Rose would be back. On the other hand, Mary could come back with her, which would complicate things again. I closed my eyes and began looking over Rose again in my mind. Every detail, every curve made me want to go find her right then. Of course I couldn't so I just sat there waiting. Suddenly, there was a knock on the door. It was Rose, but this time she was alone. I smiled and waved for her to come in. She slid in and shut the door. She gracefully walked over to my desk and took a seat.

"How was your first day?" Rose asked.

"It could of been better but I won't complain. How about yours?" I returned.

"Same as yours," Rose answered with a sly smile.

I returned her smile hoping Rose wasn't thinking what I thought she was. She leaned toward me as I thought she would and kissed me. This time I made sure to keep it under control and pulled back after a minute. Her smile was beyond breathe taking. It made me fall in love with her all over again. She leaned back in for a kiss, but this time I did not meet her. She gave me a confused look and I nodded toward the door. She stood up as a knock came from the door.

"Come in," I called.

The door opened. A tall beautiful woman stood there with some papers in her arms. I got up to get them before she dropped them all over the floor. She had her curly blonde hair pulled back into a ponytail to keep it out of her face as see worked. It helped her turquoise eyes which where covered by glasses. She slipped all the papers into my arms as noticed me for the first time. She seemed rather stunned. Then, Rose caught her eye.

"Rose, what are you doing here?" she asked.

"Mr. Hadow has been giving me tips on my writing in my spare time. If I had known you had a delivery for him I would have offered to bring for you, Miss. Waters," Rose lied.

"Yes, she is a very promising young writer. It's a pleasure to meet you, Mrs. Waters," I said while extending a hand.

She smiled and took my hand. "It's Miss. Waters, and you can call me Vivian," she corrected.

I nodded in acknowledgement. Vivian nodded for Rose to come with her. Rose got up and followed Vivian into the hall. Everytime, something just has to go wrong. I shook my head and looked up as it asking God why, before returning to my desk. The bell rang fifteen minutes later. As the class started to fill, I heard a comotion in the hall. I got up and went out to see what was happening.

A large crowd of students had gathered around a section of lockers.

They seemed to be trying to hide something from me and any other teacher within walking distance. I quickly made my way over to the comotion so that I could put a stop to it if needed. I was a good thing I did. Just as I got close enough to see what was really going on, I saw a fist pull back, ready to hit someone. I pushed through the crowd and caught the arm as it started toward its target. The crowd disbanded as they realized that I was a teacher. The student who was throwing the punch took a step back and looked at me with a smurk on his face. I turned to see that Tim was his target.

"That was a mistake, teach," the boy taunted.

"And how is that?" I questioned.

"My dad's on the school board. Stopping me just now will cost you your job," the boy laughed.

"Really! You look like you're eighteen. You still need your daddies protection? What a shame that you can't handle yourself without him. Office, now!" I ordered. The boy looked at me then looked around. No one stood behind him. Anger flashed across his face.

"This ain't over, teach," he spat.

"I think it is, bully," I mocked. With that said he turned and walked to the prinipal's office where I would go after I cleared the hall.

"Everyone, get to class," I called. The crowd began dispersing. "Tim, the asignment's on the board. Please instruct the class to hand you their homework and get started. Put the homework on my desk and get started with your own work."

"Yes, sir," Tim acknowledged.

As soon as the second bell for class rang, I made my way to the office. The boy was sitting in a chair just inside the office, acting like he had nothing to worry about. Vivian was staring at the boy from across her desk until I walked in. Her attention was then diverted to me, without discrestion.

"Mr. Hadow! Is everything alright?" Vivian asked sounding suprised to see me.

"Not quite. Is Mr. Kiddle in?" I asked.

"Yes, please go on in," Vivian insisted.

I motioned for the boy to follow me which put a look of shock on Vivian's face. He got up aggressively and pushed past me into the principal's office. I nodded to Vivian and then followed him in. Mr. Kiddle looked at both of us with the utmost surprise.

"Mr. Hadow, what brings you and Mr. Spark to my office?" Mr. Kiddle asked.

"Well, Mr. Spark here was about to," I began.

"I was stopping this punk from insulting me when this idiot stopped me and sent me here instead of," Mr. Spark interupted me to start.

"Do not interupt me!" I exclaimed with enough force to shut him up. "He was about to beat the crap out of young Tim Augustine, who is only half his size and from what I have seen, likes to be left alone. Mr. Spark here was simply being a bully and I put a stop to it."

"Mr. Hadow, I'm sure there is a perfectly good explaination for this," Mr. Kiddle tried.

"Mr. Kiddle, from the threat this young boy made, I can guess that you are afraid of his father. You are the principal, so the way I see it is that you run this school. So don't let this boy's father run it for you," I suggested.

"He has a great deal of pull over the board," Mr. Kiddle explained.

"And I can out talk anyone in this town. This is your school, not his or his son's. This boy deserves to be punished for attempting to assult another student," I commented.

"I ain't no damn boy!" Mr. Spark yelled.

"No more of that language from you young man!" Mr. Kiddle ordered.

"As for the boy comments, you aren't a man until you act like one, and being a bully is a child's game," I added.

Mr. Kiddle put Mr. Spark in detention for the remainder of the week. When I got to my class everyone was doing there work. On my desk sat three pieces of paper with stories on them. I looked at the board and saw what was added, undoubtably by Tim:

Those who do not write will not pass and will have extra work assigned each day. To those who work are the benifits of spare time.

I liked it. I walked up to the board and wrote the three names of those who did their homework and turned to the class. Everyone looked up at me hoping what Tim wrote was a joke. i smiled and looked at the three names. I handed them their papers back without even reading the first line.

"Let this be at lesson that you are not here to ride through my class without doing any work. The three who did their homework will get a hundred on it. Those who did not will be recieving a zero for their first grade. If you've changed your mind about being here you are welcome to go to the office and try getting it changed," I explained.

STURRING THINGS UP

MY DAY WENT BY SMOOTLY AFTER THAT fight. I actually got to relax. When sixth period was over I put all my grades into the computer. In total, only nine people where passing my class. I hope they learned their lesson about doing their homework. Just as I was finishing up a man walked into my classroom. He was looking over everything, then his eyes came to me. He smiled as if he had just had a large burden taken off of his shoulders.

"So you're Mr. Hadow," he said with a mocking tone.

"Yes, I am. Can I help you?" I was curious as to who this was and wanted to know what he wanted.

"You can pack your shit and leave," he replied.

"Excuss me. Who the hell are you?" I demanded.

"You don't make the demandes here. I practically own the school board so you might as well start packing. The first meeting is tomorrow and you can rest assured that I'll make sure you get fired for what you did to my son," the man snapped.

"So you're bully senior," I retorted.

"What did you call me?" Mr. Spark Sr. demanded.

"You don't demand things from me either. This is my classroom and you have no power over me. By the way, I'm not going anywhere for making your boy answer for what he did," I returned.

"Really!" Mr. Spark Sr. said with a hint of shock. "You think the board will side with you?"

"I don't think. I know. You believe that so long as you have threats,

39

you have power. Well, you can't threaten me. Unlike the people you ussually pick on, I can fight back," I corrected.

"I have more money than anyone in this town. I helped build this town," Mr.Spark Sr. started.

"Wrong. I have more money than you. You may of helped this town stay on its feet but you did not build it. If I run you out of town, they well still have me," I interupted.

"Don't you ever!" Mr. Spark Sr. began.

"You better leave before you start something you cannot finish," I snapped.

Mr. Spark Sr. didn't say another words. His anger was boiling, but my face was grave. It finally hit him that he wouldn't be able to beat me in a fight and that was what he wanted. He realized the risk and decided it wouldn't benifit him at all. True, he'd still try to get me fired, not that he'll succeed. To be honest, he didn't worry me as much as being with Rose did. Being with her could cause alot of problems for me all around. I thought about it for a second and decided to go home.

Bryan had been cleaning all day. He was behaving like we had company coming over. He probably does have company. Maybe he finally meet that special someone. I would love to see that happen for him, he really deserved it. I started preparing to leave when he suddenly took me by the ear.

"You aren't going any where," Bryan scolded.

"I haven't been a kid in a very long time, meaning I haven't been scolded in just as long," I told him.

"We worked this out just for the two of you so you are staying," Bryan explained, sort of.

"Who is we?" I asked.

The door bell rang. I looked at Bryan as he let my ear go and motioned for me to go change. Did he and Rose set me up on a date with her tonight? I blurred upstairs to get changed. I was back just as Bryan and Rose where having a seat in the livingroom.

As Rose turned to look at me, I took in the very sight of her. She wore a black skirt that went down to her knees. Her spagetti-straped shirt left a small line of skin between it and her skirt. Her shirt had a picture of a tree as it came into full bloom. Her hair was down and ran over her shoulders like a waterfall. Her eyes met mine and the magic had started agian. Her slender body came running toward me. She was more beautiful than ever. She ran right into my arms and kissed me. I kissed her back unafraid of what might happen, cause I knew my body couldn't hurt her in even the slightest bit. Bryan cleared his throat behind us. We stopped and looked at him.

"Let's not have another accident, at least not until you've had dinner," Bryan suggested with a smile.

Rose and I both laughed at the reminder. She blushed a deep shade of red which made me kiss her check to relax her. I thicked ti helped, cause her face lost some of that color. We followed Bryan into the diningroom which was already setup for us. He seated both of us and went to get the first course, which was probably all we needed. We smiled at each other as we waited for Bryan's return. Suddenly, I felt the presence of another forsaken. I looked toward the door to find Cain leaning against the doorway. Rose followed my gaze to meet Cain's. He smiled and walked toward us. I stood up to meet him.

"Cain. What a surprise?" I greeted with a hand shake.

"I decided to come by and discuss how to proceed with our problem," Cain explained.

"Maybe later tonight. Why don't you join us? It's rude to not invite you now that you're here," I offered.

"I'd like that very much. Who is your guest?" Cain inquired.

"Cain, this is Rose. Rose, this is a good friend of mine, Cain," I introduced the two of them.

"It's a pleasure," Cain said with a rather large grin on his face.

"And you as well," Rose replied.

Cain and I took seats on opposite sides of the table. He gave me a very sly look. Rose looked at both of us with a look of confusion on her face. I looked at her and grabed her hand in a reassuring way. She looked at me then quickly turned toward the kitchen as Bryan opened the door with the first course. Bryan stopped when he saw Cain. I gave him a reassuring look, so he continued with bringing the food. He looked at Cain and nodded and smiled weakly.

"I'll return with a plate for you, Cain," Bryan informed him.

"Thank you, Bryan. So where did the two of you meet, Rose?" Bryan asked.

"Well it's kind of our little secret," Rose answered.

"Really now. How exciting. I don't even remember having that kind of relationship. So how long are you planning on staying here?" Cain asked.

"Cain, you know I never know these things. Besides, this is the first time I've ever found something to keep me in any location," I replied.

"Wait! You can't be old enough to have gone too many places," Rose realized.

I gave Cain a "look at what you've done" look and turned back to Rose. She saw the exchange of glances and realized that we were hiding something from her. Cain smiled a wicked smile. Bryan returned with a plate and set it down infront of Cain and walked away. Cain began getting some food while Rose gave us the stare down. I took a deep breathe and prepared to tell her.

"He's actually quite older than he looks. If you want to be completly honest," Cain began.

"That's enough, Cain. It's my place to tell her. Rose, there are things that I didn't want to tell you, but Cain here, forced my hand. I am immortal. I have lived for over fifteen hundred years," I explained a little to see how she'd react.

"You're what!" Rose exclaimed. "That's not possible! This is some kind of joke, right, right?"

"I'm afraid not," Bryan's voice drifted from the doorway.

"But how?" Rose asked.

"You've read the Bible, correct?" Cain asked while taking another bite of food.

"Yes, I go to church every Sunday," Rose answered.

"I am Adam's son, Cain. I was forsaken to liv e forever for my crime and I can never forget what I've done. We are the forsaken," Cain explained.

Rose covered her face. I stood up and walked around to comfort her, but she just pushed my hands off of her. She stood up and walked toward the window. She stood there for a moment and just shook her head.

"I just didn't want to scare you away. I should have told you," I tried.

"Yes, you should have! Go to hell!" Rose yelled.

Rose ran out the door. I did nothing to stop her. Before Cain knew it, he was pinned against the wall. He smiled and slowly removed my hands. He pushed me back and returned to his seat. He went right back to eating as if nothing had happened. Bryan must have walked off as Rose ran out the door because he came right back through the livingroom with a shotgun and took aim at Cain. Cain blurred over to Bryan, took the gun, and blurred back to his seat.

"It's very good Bryan. You are quite the cheif," Cain complemented.

"What have you done?" I demanded.

"I forced your hand. You have been known to be slow when it comes to pushing issues with humans. I decided that I couldn't wait for your misguided conclusion. Now we know that it will take her time to calm down, but she loves you to," Cain explained.

"You call that love?" I snapped.

"Yes. She loves you. Bryan agrees, don't you, Bryan," Cain insisted.

"As much as I wanted to shoot you, you are right. Matters of the heart are complecated, even more so for you," Bryan asnwered honestly.

"So what now?" I yelled.

"You calm down and wait. There is no point in continuing in a very angry manner," Cain stated calmly.

"If he is angry, it's your fault," Bryan snapped.

"Let's not play the blame game. Besides, you've been with Shade way too long if you think you can stand up to a forsaken," Cain said with a smile and a very disapproving look at Bryan.

"It's not that I think I can so much as I won't let what you can do disuade me," Bryan pointed out.

"Enough!" I ordered with enough feriousity to shut them both up. "Cain, leave my house. Bryan, I'm sorry but it would seem that your hard work will go to waste."

With that said I retired to my room. I didn't want to see the world for a while. I could not understand why Cain did what he did, but he never went in without a plan. I had to think on it. I needed time and space. I decided to go to the cliffs to clear my head.

ATTEMPTED AMMENDS

I KNEW SHADE WOULDN'T ALLOW ME TO do this so I waited until he was gone to sneak away. It was a bold plan I must addmit, but I just had to help him. He wasn't an evil man. He had a pure heart and was very over protective of all he choose to bring into his inner circle. I was one of the few he ever brought in and I have since tried to save him from the fate he believes he deserves. No one not even Cain knows what he did to become a forsaken, but because of that one sin, he'll never be able to forgive himself. I do my best to be there for him, but for matters such as this one, he's just so stubborn.

I took his car which never bothered him since he could, as he calls it, blur faster than any car could ever move. I found Rose at the park at the base of the mountain. She did exactly what I thought she would and went any place but home. I walked toward her hoping she would let me talk to her. She looked at me and stood up so fast she got dizzy and fell. I ran over to her to help her get up, but she just pushed me away.

"Go away!" Rose yelled.

"Rose, I came to explain," I tried.

"You work for a vampire, Bryan," Rose yelled.

"He's not a vampire. He is simply forsaken. Forsaken are people who did something that God felt he had to punish them for. Shade or Mr. Hadow as you know him, has never hurt anyone unless he was saving someone in the process," I tried to explain, but she just wouldn't listen.

"He's not human, Bryan. How can you serve him?" Rose questioned.

"He's pure of heart. That is why I serve him. I see a chance to save his immortal soul," I explained.

"It's too late to save him. That's why he is forsaken, as you call it. He is beyond redemption," Rose spat.

"You love him. I can see it. He is scared that while this continues your life will be at risk, but neither of you can stay away from the other. You can't tell me anything else. You know you love him," I tried as best I could.

"I'm too young to know what love is. I'm sorry, Bryan, but I cannot help you save him. Just let it go," Rose insisted.

"Rose!" I yelled as she started to run away.

"Leave me alone!" Rose turned and screamed.

I watched as she ran back to where ever she parked. I dropped to my knees after she was out of sight. There had to be a way to fix this. I have to save Shade from a fate he does not deserve. I heard a car speed away in the distance and knew that for now I had failed. I sat there for a long while after that asking God for forgiveness for not being able to fix this. Soon enough the cold crept into my bone and I had to leave before I came down with something.

As I made my way back to the house, I thought about all the good Rose had done for Shade already. He was always happy now. I can't recall him smiling so much. He finally took a stand in his own society to make things better for the humans. He actually had a spring in his step, not that he'd notice it. I could only imagine how he felt right now.

I pulled up to the house but there was no sign of Shade anywhere. I parked the car and decided it was best to wait for him. I walked into the kitchen and began putting up all the untouched food. I was almost done when I noticed that some was missing.

"My, my, you are a most exellent cheif. All of this looks so fantasic. Let's not forget that what I've already had was the best I've ever had," came a voice from the corner.

"Cain, I thought you were gone. Did you not do enough damage?" I snapped at the vile man.

"Little human. You do not understand the ways of the forsaken. She will come back to him. I simply forced the issue," Cain stated with the utmost sincerity.

"You know nothing of the human heart, let alone a heart at all!" I yelled.

"I had a heart to feel with once, you foolish man. Yes, it killed me to kill my own brother, but sin is unstopable. I simply did the wrong sin. Now everyone sins every day. Can you imagine living while other people make the same mistake I did, and get away with it. We should be free by now, but no God condemned us for all eternity. You have no idea what we have been through. There is no redemption for our kind, no matter what you believe. There is only a final death by which all things must endure," Cain established.

Though small as he was, he seemed to tower above me as though he was a king, and I his servant. I couldn't stand this situation, but I felt helpless. I simply tried to stare back into his dark eyes, but it was too empty for my gaze to stand firm. I had to look away before I could say anything.

"I will save his soul," that was all I could manage.

"Then you are a fool who will have wasted his life on one who cannot be saved and does not need it," Cain sneered.

With that Cain was gone. He left as though he was the wind which always gave me the chills, but it was part of who they were and I was not one to ask Shade to change that for me, even though he would. I finished putting the leftovers up to pass the time hoping that Shade would return before I fell asleep.

A quiet breeze passed over me, and I knew that Shade had returned home. I finished what I was doing and went up to his room. He was sitting on his bed as quiet and as still as a statue. I took a step toward him and his gaze was on me. I stopped dead to see another empty gaze.

"Shade, she isn't gone. You still have hope," I started.

"What is hope? An illusion, I believe," Shade interupted.

"That's a lie. Hope is what keeps the world going. Hope is pure. Hope is wonderful. Hope is what keeps me alive," I tried.

"Hope is a fool's reason, and I have been a fool for a very long time. I should not have expected this to work. I should have left without letting this get beyond my control," Shade was muttering.

"You cannot control everything. Damnit, Shade, you need to snap out of this and go get her back. Yes, it might take some time. True, you might feel as though you should just give up, but you shouldn't. You can't!" I insisted.

With that I grabbed Shade and tried pulling him up. Of course, he didn't move, but I knew that would be the case. He just sat there, so I slapped him. Still, he did nothing. I went and got a baseball bat and stood infront of him.

"You leave me no choice. I won't let you give up, even if I have to resort to violence," I told him.

I took the bat and hit him right in his head. Of course, he didn't seem to be phased, but I hurt my arm. I hit him again just to express my anger. He still didn't move. It seemed as though there was nothing I could do.

I dropped the bat and decided it was time to go to bed. When I turned away from Shade, I felt a quiet breeze again and knew he was gone, for now at least. I went down to my room and got ready for bed. I changed into my night robe and put my glasses safly into there case.

As I moved toward my bed to lay down for the night, I stopped at my bed side. I knelt down to my prayers. Tonight my prayers where for the person who needed them the most and the forsaken who needed them even more:

"Heavenly Father, hear my prayer and help those I hold in my thoughts. Give them the strength to work through these trying times so that Shade's soul may be saved and returned to your glorious Book of Life. I know few more deserving of that blessing than he is, my Lord. Lord, help him find her again so that they can be whole and joyful again. Help me find to the strength to help them where you need me to. Help Shade find it in his heart to forgive the vile Cain, though I feel he does not deserve it. Lord, please help Rose find the strength to forgive Shade and myself for not telling her the truth from the very start. I pray that you help her come back to Shade for I know that with her by his side, he can find redemption, he can come home to you and your all mighty son Jesus. I pray that with Shade the world will become a better place for all of the world's peoples. I pray to you God, in Jesus's holy name, Ahmen."

THE MESS LEFT BEHIND

I MADE IT TO THE CLIFFS, FEELING cold and empty. Cain was lucky I didn't rip his head off. I couldn't believe the stunt he had just pulled. How could he. The restlessness subsided after a few moments. I had no doubt that Bryan would try to talk to Rose, but I doubted heavily that it would do any good. I heard Rose's voice echo off the cliffs, as she ordered someone to leave her alone. It was Bryan. He must have taken the car. I knew I would have to face him when I return home, if I return home. I back handed a tree cutting it in half. I pulled the stump out of the fround and threw it at the peak of the mountain. I could sense that a forsaken was close, but I knew it was just Cain, lingering to see the mess he had left behind. I took a deep breath as Cain left my territory. I took one last look at the town before I returned home. It was decided. I had to be empty forever more.

I blurred back to my house and right past Bryan, who was putting up the leftovers. I knew he would be up to talk to me as soon as he was finished, not that it would do any good. I took a seat on my bed for may be the last time. Bryan suddenly walked through my door.

"Shade, she isn't gone. You still have hope," Bryan started.

"What is hope? An illusion, I believe," I interrupted.

"That's a lie. Hope is what keeps the world going. Hope is pure. Hope is wonderful. Hope is what keeps me alive," Bryan tried.

"Hope is a fool's reason, and I have been a fool for a very long time. I should not have expected this to work. I should have left without letting this get beyond my control," I muttered.

"You cannot control everything. Damnit, Shade, you need to snap

49

out of this and go get her back. Yes, it might take some time. True, you might feel as though you should just give up, but you shouldn't. You can't!" Bryan insisted

Bryan grabbed me. I think he tried to pull me up but I couldn't really tell, I was too depressed. Suddenly, Bryan slapped me. It didn't bother me. Bryan stepped out for a moment and came back with a bat. He said something and then hit me with the bat. His face implied that he hurt hisself when he hit me, but he hit me again. He dropped the bat and started to walk away. I blurred out of the room and back to an estate I owned in Florida.

The warm sun didn't take my mind off of matters with Rose. I just had to stay away from her, at least until I can figure out what I had to do. Even the girls that overran the beach didn't help take my mind off things. I knew I would have to face this, but I just didn't know what would happen. It seemed as though the most likely out come would, unfortunatly be Rose dying. That thought alone made me regret going to Cain and trusting him with this matter as I did. It was a foolish thing I must addmit, but it seemed a logical choice. It no longer mattered, I had to fix this so that Rose lived.

It was time to speak to the council and let them in on the truth. I blurred to the council chamber. Cain was out somewhere doing God knows what. Steven, the messanger of the forsaken, was sitting in his room watching a movie. He glanced up at me when I entered, but didn't seem bothered by my presence. I glanced at the television before turning it off. He gave me a startled look.

"I need you to call the council to order within the hour. Then, I need you to keep Cain busy until I get the meeting under way," I ordered.

"Without Cain's concent?" Steven questioned.

"Did he not put me in as his epual?" I asked.

"Well, yes," Steven managed.

"Then do as I told you," I snapped.

Steven nodded in acknowledgment and blurred away to do as he was told. I looked around the room and wrinkled my nose in discust. I blurred out of the room and into the council chamber. I jumped to my doorway and waited for the other council members to arrive. As I ordered the council members where all there within the hour with the exception of Cain, who would be late if he showed up at all.

"Where is Cain, and what is this about?" Matthew, the tallest one, asked.

"This is my meeting, not his. He may be here later on if Steven can't delay him any more than a few minutes," I answered the first half of his question.

"Then please let us get this meeting under way," a hooded figure insisted.

"Very well, Skull. I called you here to correct a mistake we made long ago. The falling in love problem we were having. We were wrong. It isn't controlable," I started the meeting.

"And how have you come to this conclusion?" Knome inquired.

"I have fallen in love. She was completely unaware of who and what I was until Cain got involved. We were going to see what this could lead to before involving the council, but I feel with Cain taking matters into his own hands, I must do the same. If she is a threat to us, I will not stand in the council's way, but I do ask that Cain be punished if that does become the case. Until that becomes an apparent issue I request that she be left alone," I explained in full.

"Shade, we thank you for your honesty, and for that I will agree to your terms. Do I hear a second?" a silver haired forsaken named, Wolf answered.

"I second the motion," Skull added. "Do I hear a thrid to make it offical?"

"I," a forsaken named, Broad, motioned as he cut his finger nails with a knife.

"Then until she proves herself a threat, she is protected by this council," I announced.

The door across from me opened suddenly. Steven was thrown through the door. Cain stepped into sight as Steven hit the floor. He glared at me before scanning the room to meet the gaze of each of the council members.

"How dare you," Cain began.

"You gave me epual power, Cain. I am simply using it. You took matters into your own hands, so I returned the favor. You know me well enough to know that your little stunt will cost you," I warned, cutting him off mid-sentence.

"You should have told her immediately. Don't you think she had the right to know?" Cain challenged still.

"She had the right, when I was ready to tell her, when she was ready to know! You of all people should know what can happen when something is done too soon!" I declared with enough fury to make the chamber tremble.

"Calm yourself, Shade. We do not need a disaster, let alone the attention. You are right in being pissed at Cain, but she did have the right to know, as did we. What's done is done. There is nothing we can do about it now. Shade, you and Cain must fix this as it is the fault of both parties that we may or may not have been put into a dangerous position," the wisest of the fallen, Contempt, decided.

"I agree with Contempt on that matter," Knome piped up.

"Then as the council decides we must act," I stated.

Cain nodded in acknowledgement. The council quickly dispersed. Cain, Steven, and myself were all that remained. Steven slowly moved to get up unsure of his current predicament. I smiled a mocking smile at Cain as I leapt down to Steven's side. He looked at Cain as if Cain were about to unlease his fury upon us both, but the oddest thing happened. Cain smiled his infamous smile of success. He wanted me to push my way to the top, to his level; and I did.

"Nicely done my old friend. Let's fix your problem, before Lilith becomes an apparent threat," Cain congratulated me.

"You know me all too well, old friend," I answered with a nodd.

We both blurred out of the room, leaving Steven to pick hisself up.

THE FALSE ACCUSATION

I WENT HOME TO FIND BRYAN SOUND asleep in his bed. There was a note with my name on it in the kitchen. I thought it was from him at first, but the hand writing didn't match. It wasn't Rose's or anyone I coul think of, so I examined it before reading it.

Hey sexy,

You weren't home and your BUTLER was asleep so I wrote you this note since you didn't lock your door when you left. I'm here for you waiting for you to come make me yours. Please don't take too long, I do have a curfew that I can be only so late for. I'm waiting. We aren't in school anymore.

Mary

I gave a sigh of disappointment. This girl didn't seem to be catching that I wasn't interested in her. I threw the note away and went up stairs to get her out of my house. I got to my room, but it was empty. There was no sign of a struggle or a very long wait for what seemed to be a very impatient girl. This puzzled me, I have to addmit, but I just shrugged it off and got ready for the day to come. I had alot to do and only part of it dealt with my classes.

I picked out my best suit to change into. I went to my hiden flower garden and picked a dozen roses(ironic I know). I blurred to the school and broke into her locker to put them in. It was a good thing this school was so low-tech that they hadn't installed cameras yet. I blurred back home to finish getting ready. It seemed like a lifetime went by as I slowly got ready. My shower, which only took an hour, felt like it took over a year.

My thoughts kept flying back to her; then to Cain and how he planned to help me. Cain worried me a little, but I could handle anything he would do. The sun finally began to rise into the sky. It was clear that I wasn't the only one up, but the comotion was rather unsettling. I grabbed my papers and laptop before going down stairs. I grabbed the keys to the car and waved to Bryan as I slipped out the door.

The drive was very odd indeed. All of the parents seemed to be in a hurry, buzzing around looking for something. Even stranger was the fact that as I drove by, each and every one of them stoped and looked right at me as if I was guilty of something. I got to the school building and the students were in a state of panic. Something had happened and I needed to find out what. Vivian was standing at the doors directing students to go straight to their homcrooms so I thought it best to ask her.

"Vivian, what's going on? The town's in an uproar. What happened?" I asked concerned with what the answer would be.

"Mr. Hadow, Mr. Kiddle wants all the teachers in their classrooms. I can't say anymore. I'm sorry," Vivian answered as best she could.

I nodded my head and walked past her. I went straight to my classroom. I shut the door behind me and crossed the room to my desk. It took me longer than it should have to realize that I wasn't alone. I turned to find Rose sitting in the corner, the roses I gave her in her hand. Concern spread across my face like wildfire.

"What is it, Rose? What happened last night, that sent the town into a frenzy?" I asked.

She shook her head refusing to look at me. I took a step toward her, but she flinched. I stoped and steped back. She suddenly looked at me, her eyes were overflowing with tears. She was questioning and accusing me with her eyes, but she couldn't look at me for very long. She put her head into her knees and began crying. Without warning, Cain was right next to me.

"Shade, you need to go," Cain said with a crumpled note in his hand. It was the one Mary left me.

"What happened?" I demanded.

"A girl never returned home last night. A Mr. Spark is pointing the finger at you. They have launched a full scale investigation into the matter with you as their prime and only suspect," Cain explained,

"Foolish girl. If the note wasn't enough proof for you, she was at my

54

house last night. We were in a meeting. She was gone by the time I got home. Rose are you ok?" I inquired.

"Why should I believe you didn't take her to get back at me," Rose cried.

"Because in all the years I have known Shade, he has never been the vengeful type until I tried to seperate the two of you, but he aimed at me," Cain spoke before I had the chance.

I blurred over to Rose's side. She flinched away from me, but relaxed once I had her in my arms. I craddled her while I tried to figure out what to do about this.

"She told me she was trying to get you to sleep with her. She said you wouldn't even give a glance of interest. Why?" Rose asked.

"We don't fall in love. On a very rare occasion, we do. It happens at first sight. There is no explaining it, no excaping it. It becomes perminant. I fell for you," I answered her.

She buried herself into my arms. I held her close wanting to comfort her as much as possible. Cain walked up to us. He put a hand on my shoulder to get my attention. I too could hear the police heading this way. Cain was telling me to send her to class to keep our secret. I nodded in response. I slowly slide away from Rose until I could see her face.

"Rose, my love, the police are coming. I need you to go to class. Cain I need you to leave. I love you, Rose," I said softly.

"I love you too," Rose replied.

Cain blurred out into town to get information about the disappearance. Rose slowly stood up. I held her steady and walked her to the door. I understood that Mary was her best friend, and that unlike any of the friends I've had in centuries, they were very close. I shut the door behind her and returned to my work to await the coming injustice. I didn't have to wait long. About five minutes after Rose left, Mr. Kiddle and a few police officers entered the room. I greeted them with a curious smile.

"Mr. Kiddle, what is the uproar about? I asked Miss Waters, but she said that you had sworn her to silence," I asked knowing what the answer would be.

"Rose's friend Mary didn't return home last night. Have you seen her?" Mr. Kiddle inquired.

"I'm afraid I haven't. Is there any way I can help?" I asked knowing that they intended to arrest me.

"Mr. Hadow, we found a pair of her underwear under your bed. You're going to have to come with us," the short officer informed me.

"She went to my house with the intention of sleeping with me. I've turned her down several times here at the school. I wasn't home when she was there. By the time I got home, she was gone," I tried to explain.

"BULL SHIT!" I heard from behind the cops.

"Mr. Spark, please, you shouldn't be here," the officer insisted.

"I want to see justice delivered to that fucking prick!" Mr. Spark yelled trying to push through the cops.

They detained Mr. Spark while they arrested me. I didn't fight them, even though I could win with my hands behind my back. In this situation I needed to coroporate, and that's exactly what I planned to do. I knew Cain would fix everything like only he knows how. Rose watched them walk me down the halls. Tears just kept running down her face. I started to resist so I could comfort her, but the the end result would be far worse than a few hours of suffering. As they took me out the front doors I fealt a third Forsaken close by. It wasn't Lilith or any of the council members. This one was a stranger to me.

Cain was outside. He made sure he caught my eye and nodded toward Mr. Spark Jr. which kind of surprised me. I thought it was Mr. Spark Sr. that planted the evidence. Cain stepped forward and demanded the cops stop and release me. Both Mr. Spark Jr. and Sr. ran toward the cops in protest. Cain took a camera out of his pocket and hit a few buttons before showing it to the police. It was a collection of girls underwear with the pair marked as Mary's missing. Rose didn't have a place on the wall which made me smile inside.

"This is in Mr. Spark's closet. Spark Jr. stole it and placed it at Mr. Hadow's house to put the blame on him. This doesn't explain what happened to Mary but it does clear Charles. Now realease him," Cain ordered.

The short officer uncuffed me and then slammed a pair on each of the Mr. Sparks. He arrested Junior for tampering with evidence, and Senior for several accounts of rap. I shook Cain's hand, but Cain pulled me into a hug. The crowd around the school cheered now that the Spark family had no more control in town. Cain turned and shook the hands of all the officers involved and offered his services. He glanced at me and I knew what he had discovered. The third Forsaken was the real kidnapper.

I went back into the school and found Rose. She was in my room looking over my stuff. When she saw me enter the room her face just exploded with excitment. She ran right into my arms and kissed me. I moved her a step back and looked over my shoulder as two students went by. I turned back to her and smiled. Her smile faded slightly as she remembered that her friend was still missing. I sat her down in one of the desks and knelt down infront of her.

"I know who took Mary, but the police cannot handle this matter. Mary may already be dead and for that I am truely sorry," I began.

There was a knock on the door. I looked up to see Vivian standing there with a very jeolous look on her face. I knew what she was thinking and I didn't like what she probably would do.

"Well I wanted to be the first to congratulate you on being found innocent, but it looks as though your favorite student beat me to it," Vivian said in a very threatening tone.

"She was in here working on her writing, trying to take her mind off of Mary. It wasn't working. I'm trying to calm her down. Thank you for coming by. Are the classes still on today or is it possible for me to go join the search?" I asked trying to make her lose her train of thought, but I failed.

"They have all been cancelled. I'll let Mr. Kiddle know that you've gone to join the search. Happy hunting," Vivian answered mockingly.

THE HENCHMAN

I GATHERED MY THINGS AND RETURNED TO my house to drop off my things. Bryan was shut up in his room so I left him a note telling him what was going on. Then I went back to town to offer my help which they gladly accepted. I suggested allowing me a one or two others search my land since she was there last night. Cain and one of the senior volunteered to be my help. Cain knew what I planned to do so when we got back to the mountain, Cain and the student went one way while I went after the other Forsaken. As soon as they were out of sight I blurred up to the mountain's peak where the Forsaken was waiting.

The Forsaken was a slim man with black hair and a dark complexion. He looked to be of Aisan descent. He was toned, that was obvious with his tight shirt, but something wasn't right. He was too weak to be challenging me like this. What was his game? There was only one thing to do. I stepped out into the open so that he could see me. A smile stretched across his face.

"Who the hell are you?" I demanded.

"A friend of a friend. The name's Ra. You came here for the girl? How strange? She doesn't want to go home anymore," Ra said with a mocking smile.

"What the hell have you done to her? Is this some kind of game to you?" I snapped.

"Not anymore. You came here just as I was told you would, but I was not told what would happen when I saw her. I will not give her up," Ra returned.

"You've fallen for her," I stated what was becoming the very obvious.

"Yes. As I said you are not taking her back. She is mine now. That bitch can't have her either, even if it gets her close to you," Ra snapped.

"Ra, she has to go back to her family, at least for now. I know how you feel. but if you don't control your emotions you will die," I tried, but he just smiled that mocking smile at me.

"I am in control and she wants to stay with me. I don't care what you think you have to do. I know what I will do," Ra declared.

"Then why are you waiting here for me like this?" I inquired.

"To deliver a message for that bitch Lilith. She is coming to kill you if she can't have you. Now leave and forget that Mary was ever alive," Ra ordered.

"I cannot. You are out of control and for that I must stop you, before something bad happens in the world," I stated with enough force to make Ra stop.

Ra turned toward me. He was no longer smiling. Rage filled his eyes as he took an offensive stance and prepared to fight me, to the death if nessasary. I tensed up just in time to catch him as he charged into me. The force from the collision shook the whole mountain and undoubtably the town as well. Ra threw his knee into my gut, knocking me off balance so that he could launch me into the trees. I grabbed a rock and pulled myself to a stop as he came bounding through the trees to hit me again. This time he leapt into the air to bring his fist down upon me. I caught his arm and slammed him head first into the rock. I then threw my knee into his side with enough force to finish the rock and crack one of his ribs. Ra cried out in pain and punched me dead in the face. I stumbled back enough for him to turn and tackle me. I threw my knees up and grabbed his sides to flip him over me. I rolled on top of him and punched him in the face. He kneed me in the back which knocked me off of him. He quickly got up and wraped his arms around my back. I reached between my legs and grabbed one of his. I pulled his leg hard enough to knock us both down. The force made him let go of me so I rolled off of him and took a defensive stance.

Ra stood up and charged me again. This time I threw him through two or three trees. I ran after him and before he could get up I slammed into him. I heard another crunch as my body stopped against his. He fell back over and tumbled down the mountain a few feet. I was on top of him before he had a chance to move. I grabbed his head but he threw me over himself. I rolled back onto my feet as he speared his shoulder into me. This time it was my rip that cracked. I grabbed hold of him and twisted in order to slam him down into the mountain. We fell into an underground cavern. He was up just as quickly as I was. Ra grabbed a rock and launched it at me. I blurred to the side but he slammed into me again. This time I put him into a head lock so that his head rammed into the rock behind me. I let him go and brought my elbow down between his shoulder blades, breaking his back. He fell to the ground unable to stand.

"I tried to help you, Ra. You should have listened to me. Now you must die. I am sorry," I told him.

I once again grabbed his neck. I snapped it and then ripped his head off. I threw his head across the cavern and threw a match on his body to destroy his remains. I took a seat on a nearby rock to show my respect as his body turned to ash. When the fire was ready to go out I went back to the mountain peak. Mary was asleep about twenty yards from where I found Ra. She looked so peaceful so I was careful not to wake her as I ran her down the hill. She smelt of whiskey which made a cover up very easy. I told everyone that she must have gotten lost and that there was no one around when I found her. She was unharmed so no one doubted me. She didn't even remember Ra.

When he got a chance, Cain pulled me off to the side for the full story. I gave him a look to tell him not now and he nodded in compliance. I went to see Rose who was still next to Mary in the hospital. Rose and Mary both smiled. Mary was told about the collection that Cain found and was a little ashamed that she was part of it. She looked to me for forgiveness, but I told her it wasn't mine to give. Rose kissed Mary on the forehead before following me out the door. We walked outside so we could talk.

"It was a Forsaken, but he, like I, fell in love. He wouldn't have harmed her, but he wasn't bringing her back. I had to kill him," I explained.

"She remembers, but she can't and won't tell anyone. She doesn't want any man anymore either. Just like me," Rose informed me.

"The falling in love works on both of us. I want you to know that I will love you until the day I die," I told her.

"I know, I know. I will too, though my life won't be as long as yours," Rose returned.

Rose took a step forward. I kissed her like I already have, but it still took me completely by surprise. Every moment with her would be the best moment I ever had for as long as she is next to me. She pulled away very slowly and looked at me. I smiled softly as I looked into her beautiful blue eyes. Unfortunately, I was about to have to leave her, at least for a little while, an unbarrable little while. Her look turned from blissfully happy to curious. She pulled back and gave me a you're busted look.

"What?" I asked wondering what she was doing.

"You're going after Lilith aren't you?" Rose asked. A shock ran through my body as she said Lilith's name. How on earth did she know about Lilith?

"How do you know of her?" I asked immediately.

"Mary said that Ra was talking about her infatuation with you," Rose said with a question mark face.

"She wants me to join her in taking the world for ourselves. I have to stop her. She will come for you if I don't. Ra was just her henchman. She is the real threat. Please, my beautiful Rose, stay out of harms way or I will die a thousand times over," I explained and pleaded.

"I promise," Rose whispered in my ear as she gave me one last hug before returning to Mary.

I watched her walk back into the hospital longing to be able to go with her. I turned and walked out of sight. When I was sure no one could see me, I blurred back to the house where Cain sat waiting. I explained what happened as only a Forsaken could, with every detail. He nodded his head here and there, but never said a word. We both knew what had to be done.

"I'll go call the council and prepare them for what has to be done. At least Rose is safe," Cain stated.

"Indeed," I replied.

No sooner had the words poured out of my mouth did the phone begin ringing. It was Rose's mother. Rose was missing and her mother was hoping she had simply gone with me. I regretfully informed her that I left Rose at the hospital and would go out to search for her. I got off the phone and turned to Cain.

"I will help you find her," Cain said without hesitation.

"No. Lilith has her. You need to let the council know. We have to be ready to clean her up. I will go stall her and if need be, I will fight her, even if I have to die," I told him with a tone that even he could not disobey.

Cain bowed his head and blurred away. I turned to find Bryan in the door way. His face looked grim. He steped to the side with a nod and a look of regret. I touched his shoulder as I walked by. I got to the door and blurred away to fight for the love I couldn't live without.

LILITH'S KINGDOM

I BLURRED TO A RUN DOWN BUILDING that was once a palace, Lilith's palace. This was once the center of her kingdom, a kingdom long forgotten by all but the Forsaken. This was our kingdom.

The night I met Lilith, she was throwing an extrodinary party here at her palace. She named herself the Queen of our kind, but even then, the council was preparing to take power. I came with Judas, who was killed some time ago for what Lilith is trying to do. He had faith that I was going to be a very powerful friend so he wanted to bring me into the world right. I was still young and very foolish. That's what caught Lilith's eye. She got me away from Judas so that she could have me for herself, but I wasn't interested. That's why Cain walked right into Lilith to distract her so I could get away. Cain and I have been friends ever since.

I walked up the wheathered steps to the front enterance that no longer has a door. Without her servants, Lilith's palace went to hell, which is where I plan to send her. I entered the house for the second time since I was born into this damned world and to my best guess Lilith was standing there waiting for me, almost as she was all those years ago. A victorious smile covered her face from ear to ear. She straightened up to give herself a look of power.

"I knew you would be mine from the very first time I saw you, I just knew. Now look at you, back in my house," Lilith said as though I was begging for forgiveness.

"I am not yours. I came to send you straight to hell. You took her and I will have her back," I spat.

"You have to kill me to even leave this room. And I won't tell you were she is. You will both die if you try to fight me," Lilith toyed.

"I will save her, even if I die in the process," I declared.

"Then you will die, here and now, by my hands, the hands you should have had your whole life!" Lilith promised.

Lilith's body began to crack and expand. She was changing her shape, but to what? I didn't know or care, she was dead. I shifted me stance to the defensive as she took her new form. She was a werewolf. Lilith wasn't the only one to learn how to shapeshift but she was far stronger now than she was moments ago, but I too had a secret. Lilith stood before me a monster who aimed to destroy me and everything I was, but I wouldn't let her. My mind was set and that was where my true power stayed.

"You pushed me into this, Shade," Lilith growled.

"And you forced my hand,Lilith," I returned as she launched herself toward me.

From nowhere a wave of power erupted, aimed at Lilith. The power knocked her back into the stairs. She stood up slowly. An ear-peircing growl filled the room. More power sent cracks through the walls as I too prepared for a fight. Lilith steped out of the reckage of her stairs.

"What the hell was that!" Lilith exclaimed.

"I can launch power out of my mind. Cain is the only one until you who knew I had this power. You cannot win this fight, Lilith," I told her.

"We shall see," Lilith prompted.

Lilith started forward. I sent a wave at her, but she started to zigzag across the room. After missing her for the third time, I sent a wave that covered the whole area she was running in. She slide back a few feet and then launched herself back into attack mode. This time when I sent a wave of power at her, she leapt over it and right into me. She tackled me hard throwing us both back into the wall behind me. She drew back to slash my throat with her claws, but I sent another wave of power to throw her off of me. She quickly recovered and launched herself back at me. I put up a shield that stoped her about two feet from where I stood.

She pushed back and landed thirty yards away. She slowly straightened up to look at me.

"You're more powerful than I expected. That mind power is very useful. Are you sure you won't reconcider joining me. I know we could take this world by storm. I'll let her live," Lilith tempted.

"I know you too well to believe anything you say. You will kill her when my usefullness is over. I think killing you now would be a much better solution," I answered honestly. Lilith would kill Rose, one way or the other. I had no intention of giving her that chance.

"Too bad. You were a force to be reconded with, but soon, you'll be dead. I will be the queen once again, and this time, no one will over throw me," Lilith roared.

I launched a wave of power at her, but she leapt to the side and grabbed the wall. She ran across the wall narrowly dodging the waves of power I threw at her that destroyed the wall behind her like dominoes. She leapt onto the ceiling and launched herself on top of me. The force sent us through the floor into the cellar. With an explosion of power, I sent Lilith back through the hole. She landed gracefully and waited for me to follow her up. I ran to stand underneath her and then jumped through the floor, catching her off guard. I slammed her into the ground, which sent another ripple through the floor. She kicked me hard, and sent me flying across the room. I got up just in time to divert her next attack. She flew back a few feet, but landed on her feet. She croached down ready to find another opening. I had no intention of leting her.

Another presence pulled at my mind, but only just. It was my backup, but he didn't show hisself. It was as though he was looking for something or rather someone. Thank you, Cain. With Steven looking for Rose, I stood a chance of surviving this battle without losing her. I let another explosion of power burst, which caused the whole house to rattle. A few peices even fell down. Lilith looked around wildly, then turned her gaze toward me.

"If my home falls, your love dies!" Lilith screamed.

"Then let us all die for the sake of stoping you," I spat.

I let another explosion happen. This time the house trembled violently. Lilith's fear became clear in her eyes. I had her right where I wanted her. A smile filled my face for the first time since I entered this house. I was in control and now Lilith knew it. She looked from place to place wildly as the building started to come down. With one last attempt, she pleaded with me.

"Please, I will stop this! I'll give the girl back to you!" Lilith screamed.

"It's too late, besides, you'd kill me first chance you got. I can't trust you, so I have to kill you," I declared.

I felt Steven move away from here. He found her. I had nothing left to worry about, I simply had to kill Lilith. My smile deepened as I sent another wave that caused the roof to start caving in. Panic filled Lilith's eyes as she tried to make for a way out. I cut her off at every pass. Finally, I caught up to her. I pulled a dagger out of my shirt and ran her through. She dropped to her knees and returned to her human form. I steped infront of her, the building coming down all around us, and took her head without a word. As the whole roof gave way, I blurred out of the house to watch the fall of a once great power.

No one would miss her or this place, this forgotten hell. The community would be happy to have the land back. As for the remaining Forsaken, we would be happy to be done with the bitch who wanted to rule us all.

"Have fun in hell, Lilith," I whispered as the last of the building fell.

IT'S ALL OVER

"Lilith is dead," I told Cain, Steven, and Rose.

"Thank God," Rose blurted.

"Indeed. I will take care of her affairs. Steven," Cain said.

"Yes," Steven replied.

"Prepare a cover story for what happened to the house. We don't want anybody near there until our clean up crew is done with the remains. Shade, you are my best friend and partner in all our lives have and will entail, but right now we need to celebrate," Cain said with a great smile.

"Please remember that I am a minor, and that I want Shade, here, ready to be with me tonight," Rose interjected with a sly smile as she cuddled into my side.

A smile breached my face. "You heard her, but we don't get drunk," I said with a laugh.

We all started laughing. It was strange how even with someone's death on our shoulders, we could still laugh and have a good time. For the Forsaken, this was not uncommon, but for Rose, a human, it didn't fit. I guess now that she was part of our world, death was something she would have to get use to. My biggest problem was how to tell her parents that we would be getting married one day in the not too distant future. I need to worry about one thing at a time, and the first thing to do was to pick out a ring and figure out how to propose. Then the two of us could figure out what to do from there. Till then, I finally had a reason to enjoy life for the first time in centuries, I planned on enjoying every minute of it.

RELICS OF THE PAST

THE YEAR CLOSES

I<small>T'S BEEN MONTHES SINCE</small> L<small>ILITH</small> <small>MADE HER</small> attempt at the throne of the Forsaken. There has been a series of unexplainable events that have us Forsaken in an uproar. Cain's spy, Mimic, has discovered that over the last two years ten of our kind have disappeared. There were no traces to be found, not one. They either, choose to leave in this manner or, have been disposed of. Cain and myself are leaving in a few weeks to investigate, but till then this is a time of celebration.

Her parents may have threw the biggest fit I had ever seen, but Rose has agreed to marry me. Cain is to be my best man at the wedding. First, however, I have to let Rose graduate. The graduation cerimony is tomorrow night, and I can't wait for her to be in my arms, forevermore. Bryan has been busier than ever, trying to prepare the wedding, which makes him so happy that he's basicly glowing. My life has become a fairy tale, and I for one, hope it stays this way, but I know nothing lasts forever.

"Hey beautiful," I called as I approached Rose and her friends.

"Why thank you, but I think Rose might get jeolous," Mary stepped up to say.

"And you know full well that I only have eyes for Rose," I corrected.

"We know, we know. Mary just wishes you would have given her the time of day. Besides, Mary's not intersted in anybody anymore," Alice piped up.

"See, I told you that she still liked to mess with you," Rose finally spoke.

It had only been a few hours since I last saw her, but it always felt like a life time. Every time I saw her, my heart soared. Every time I heard her, my brain went into hyper-drive. Every time I held her, I felt more alive than I ever had. Rose was my one and only reason to be alive, my one and only reason to want redemption for the crime I did against that man.

"Very true. You did warn me, but you know how serious I have to be some times when other women say stuff like that. It's only fair, don't you agree?" I agreed.

"Other women are always trying to get you into their beds. Mary was joking. Besides, why should you even worry about other women trying. They should know by now that they will never succeed," Rose challenged.

"Very true," I answered. Rose and Cain were the only two in the world who could win an arguement with me. Rose because I loved her too much to fight her, and Cain because he was very hard to argue with.

"Guess who she finally picked to be her maid of honor?" Mary prompted.

"You," I quickly answered with a mocking smile.

"She told you!" Mary said in an accusing manner.

"No, I always knew she would," I added to save Rose from the accusing look.

"Oh," Mary said as she snapped out of it.

The bell rang for the student and teachers to get to class. I gave Rose a sad fairwell look as she turned to go to class. With me being a teacher and her a student, we were forbidden to touch inside the school building until after she graduated. I understood it and often times had to be the voice of reason so we wouldn't get into trouble. I turned and walked the very short three feet to my classroom. Mr. Kiddle was there looking over my things. He turned with a shock as he realized that I was there.

"Ah Mr. Hadow, this is a big month for you, isn't it?" Mr. Kiddle asked in greetings.

"Yes it is," I said with a laugh. "What can I do for you?"

"I came to see if you were going to stay and continue teaching next year," Mr. Kiddle said modestly.

"If you would have, then yes I would love to. The kids took awhile to warm up to me, expecailly with that attempt at blaming me for Mary's disappearance at the begining of the year. Things should go much smoother next year," I answered hoping that he wasn't here to tell me I was no longer welcome to teach here due to the parents being worried about me marrying one of the students from here.

"I'm glad to hear it, and I look forward to working with you further. Will you be attending the graduation tomorrow night?" Mr. Kiddle asked in relief.

"Yes, and my friend Cain will be there as well," I added.

"Very good, Cain is a very intellectual man that I enjoy debating with, even if I do always lose," Mr. Kiddle said with a slight chuckle.

The day went by very quickly. That night still didn't seem to get there fast enough for me. Rose finally got to the house and launched herself into my arms. I kissed her gently and set her down. Cain came down the stairs and gave her a quick hug as if she were his sister, which is how he saw her. Bryan ran into the room as best he could to hug her. Bryan was sick a few monthes ago. The doctors were surprised by his recovery and even more surprised that he returned to work, even though I wouldn't allow him to do anything that could hurt him. Unfortunatly, Bryan never fully recovered. He now had a limp in his left leg. It sickened me that I could do nothing, but the man is so stubborn that he wouldn't let me take care of him, so for now I had him worrying about the wedding only.

"How do you feel, Bryan?" Rose asked.

"Fit as a fiddle," Bryan answered with a brillant smile.

"So he says. You really should take it easy," Cain stated.

"And to think that I use to think you were a villian," Bryan said with a laugh.

"We both were at a time," I added.

"Sins are made to be forgiven," Bryan said shortly.

"Bryan, you are taking the night off to have movie night with us," I basicly ordered.

"But I have so much to do," Bryan tried.

The door bell rang. Cain cut Bryan off so that Rose and I could drag him into the livingroom. Cain got the door. Rose and sat Bryan in the recliner so he would be too comfortable to get up. Cain entered the livingroom alone with a puzzled look on his face. I looked at him with a question mark face. He motioned for me to forget it so I did. We spent the whole night watching monster flicks.

Soon it was the day Rose and I had been waiting for. He parents helped us pack her things and move them to the house before it was time for the graduation. We had everything moved in and set up (mostly thanks to me and Cain) by three, which gave us just over two hours to get ready for graduation. We all piled into my car and insisted that Rose rode with her family as that was the way of things. We all arrived safe and sound with half an hour to spare.

The ceremony was fantastic, however something, rather someone, caught my eye. There was a man sitting opposite of me in a hooded cloak. He seemed to be ignoring the ceremony to stare at me. I couldn't give him my full attention since the love of my life was about to graduate high school and step into the real world, with me at her side of course. I watched her get her deploima and returned my gaze to the cloaked figure, but he was gone.

Rose ran into my arms after the ceremony was over and they were free of the school. He parents told her how proud they were and wished her the best of luck. She promised that they would see her often and that they shouldn't act as though she was leaving them forever. I held her close to me as she waved a farwell to some of her friends who choose not to stay for the wedding. She turned to me suddenly, and gave me her "I'm ready" look. I picked her up and carried her to the car. We laughed the whole way with Cain and Bryan on our heels. We got home that night and went straight to bed.

THE THREAT

THE NEXT MORNING WAS TO BE A joyous day to prepare for the wedding I have longed to have for centuries. However, an early message caught my attention when Bryan described the one who left it. It was the man I saw last night at graduation. I quickly ripped the envelope away and read the note.

> I know who and what you are. For you to marry this girl is a sin that I cannot allow. I will kill you vile creature, damned to live forever. For your mis-deads against my home and family over a hundred years ago. And so now that I have found you, everything you hold dear, I will rip them from you as you have done to me. I will see you very soon, Shade.

The note had no name of any kind. I began trying to pull any memory of an event at that time that would have left me an enemy. I could think of none. What was this man talking about and how the hell was he still alive to take revenge anyway? These were questions that I had to answer and soon, because nothing would come between me and Rose. I promised her that after Lilith kidnapped her. I went up to the room I leant to Cain to find it perfectly empty, which killed my idea of asking his opinion of the threatening note.

Rose walked up behind me and hugged me as best she could. I pulled her infront of me and kissed her gently. She wrapped herself around me and raised one leg. I smiled as she began kissing my neck. She knew it tickled me, and did it just to see me smile. A cough from the stairs made us both jump and take a step back. Cain was standing there with a curious look on his face. I gave him a questioning look so that he would tell me what was on his mind.

"It's a good thing that I did leave on business last night otherwise I would have been trapped in my room just then. Did you need something or were you unable to make it to your room?" Cain asked with an evil grin.

"Actually, I do need to talk to you about a private matter. Rose, do you mind?" I asked her with a kiss.

"You know what we have to do today, so I don't see why I should stop you from the duties you have with the Forsaken. Love you," Rose replied and went down stairs.

Cain stepped to the side and let her pass. He gazed after her for a moment as if he were contimplating something. I took a few quick steps forward to catch his attention. He didn't even flinch as I put my hand on his right shoulder. He simply watched the door as Rose walked out of it.

"She'll be my wife and you are staring at her as if you were in love," I stated.

"Not quite. I'm thinking about what it would be like to have what you have. It's a wonderful dream," Cain said still in a daze.

"It may very well come to pass, old friend. The matter I needed to speak with you is this note," I said as I pulled it out of my pocket.

That is when Cain snapped back into reality. He took the note and read it quickly. He folded it up and stuck it in his pocket. He looked back down stairs then nodded toward his room. I followed him quietly. He shut the door behind me and looked at me with a very concerned look on his face.

"We believe that there have been more Forsaken since you and Breethus. This, man, is most likely one of those who have become us without showing themselves. What ever crime he feels you have done against him is most likely what caused him to become a Forsaken. We need to figure out what happened that has him set on you. Then and only then can we resolve this. We need him alive to discover why he was Forsaken so that our people can either survive or fade away. Do you understand?" Cain explained.

"So long as we can stop him, I will not harm him, Cain. You have my word," I answered.

"Very good. Thank you, my friend," Cain returned.

"No need, Cain. Now we have a few short hours before the big event.

I think it is time for us to get ready. We are two very important parts of this joyous day," I stated.

"Yes, I agree. Let's get ready so we can finish with the preparations," Cain agreed.

I nodded and returned to my room. I found the tuxido laying on my bed. I quickly put it on. I stayed in the room for awhile longer to make it seem like I took longer getting dressed. When I felt I had been gone long enough, I steped out of my room. Rose's mother was there. She looked me over.

"Mrs. Augusteine, can I help you with something?" I inquired.

"Take care of my daughter," Mrs. Augusteine said.

"With everything I am," I informed her.

"And forgive my husband," Mrs. Augusteine added.

"For what, Mrs. Augusteine?" I asked wondering if she knew I hit him with a rock at the begining of the school year.

" You'll see. I'm sorry," Mrs. Augusteine said as she walked away.

As Mrs. Augusteine got to the top of the stairs, Tim walked passed her. He gave her a funny look and continued toward me. I smiled as he turned back toward me.

"Hey, Tim, you excited?" I asked.

" I'm happy for you two. Rose didn't need to stay in that house too much longer. Unfortunately, I'm still stuck there," Tim answered.

"It won't be too long before you get out," I tried.

"Still too long for me. I think dad is planning something," Tim told me.

"Your mother was acting a bit strange," I said calmly.

"Please be careful today," Tim begged.

" Will do," I returned with a smile.

Tim smiled and went back down the stairs. Cain's door opened. He steped out and turned toward me. He looked concerned. I walked toward him. Bryan walked up the stairs to check on us.

"Is everything ok?" Bryan asked.

"Cain?" I inquired.

"I just got a message. One of the council was just assassinated. As soon as the wedding is over, I have to go investigate," Cain explained.

"I'll join you," I offered.

"No, you have a honeymoon to take care of," Cain insisted.

"If you think you can handle it," I agreed.

"I can. You enjoy your wife," Cain stated with an evil grin.

"It's almost time," Bryan stated.

Cain and I both nodded. Bryan turned and headed down the stairs. Cain and I followed Bryan down the stairs and through the kitchen into the back yard. There were white chairs lined up down my yard. I had a gazebo built just for this occasion. Everyone in town was in my back yard. I never had so many people in my home. Cain and I walked down the isle greating everyone that was on the end. Bryan turned and went back into the house. Cain and I got to the gazebo and got into our positions.

The music started playing. I couldn't help but to be filled with joy. A smile spread across my face as the bridesmaids started down the isle. The last bridesmaid started down the isle. My stomach was in my throat as rose should have started down the isle. She wasn't there. A loud noise came from the house. The crowd started whispering. Rose's voice echoed out of the house. Cain and I both ran down the isle and into the house. Mr. Augusteine was trying to chase Rose around the table.

"You think you can do what you want just because he wants you. You are MY daughter and you will not marry that man. You will do as I tell you. Now let's go home," Mr. Augusteine yelled.

"No, I love him, and I am going to marry him....... today," Rose yelled back.

"I'll kill you if you try!" Mr. Augusteine exclaimed.

Cain grabbed Mr. Augusteine and pinned him down. I ran to Rose and held her tightly. Several guests started gathering at the doorway. Cain dragged Mr. Augusteine toward the front. I motioned for him to stop.

"Rose, what do you want to do?" I asked her.

"I want to marry you," Rose sobbed. "And I want my father to watch."

"Mr. Augusteine, will you calm down?" I asked.

"Never will I give her permission to marry you!" Mr. Augusteine snarled.

"Then you leave me no choice. Cain tie him to a chair. You will watch this wedding for your daughter's sake, Mr. Augusteine," I decided.

Cain smiled as he dragged Mr. Augusteine out the back door and through the crowd.

I kissed Rose's forehead. Rose snuggled into me. Tim walked in and offered his hand to Rose. She smiled and took it. I nodded to him and walked back to the gazebo. Cain had just finished tying Mr. Augusteine to a chair on the front row when the music started back. Cain ran to my side as Tim and Rose started down the isle.

This time I looked at Rose and took all of her in. I didn't take time to look at her when her father caused the commotion. Her white veil tried to hide her long black hair. Her slender form glided gracefully down the isle. I was in heaven, though I would never go there in reality. I took in every detail as she came to my side, to be mine forever. For the first time in centuries, I felt a little faint. Her beautiful white dress with flower designs hugged her frame perfectly. At last, she pulled up her veil. First, her thin rose red lips came into sight. Then, her alluring blue eyes captured me. Her soft skin cried out to me. Her smell over powered me. I think I found something even better than heaven could ever be.

I barely noticed anyone or anything as the cerimony proceeded. I don't even know how I knew to say "I do" at the right time. Finally, I heard "You may kiss the bride." I pulled Rose close and kissed her with everything I was. She returned the favor as best she could. It seemed like forever had passed when we stoped. Most of the crowd cheered as we turned to face them. Mrs. Augusteine untied her husband. Cain smiled as he disappeared in the crowd. Everyone made their way toward the area set up for the reception. Rose and I brought up the rear of the bunch.

Everyone had a good time, after Mr. and Mrs. Augusteine left that is. Since Cain left and he was my best man, I let Tim do the toast (he drank grape juice). When Rose and I cut the cake, I smeared a little bit of frosting on her upper lip so she smeared the whole peice on my face. Even I had a blast, despite the threatening note that was hidden in his dresser drawer.

Unfortunatly, the party was cut short. A scream came from around front as the first of the guests were leaving. It caused a greater commotion than when Mr. Augusteine started with Rose earlier. Then, I heard something that made my heart stop.

"Call 911!" someone yelled.

I glanced at Rose who wore a look of horror as she heard those words. She nodded for me to go ahead. I let go of her hand leaving her with Tim. I rushed through the house and out the front door. Everyone was staring above me. I looked up to see Bryan hanging on a cross. The cross was nailed to the second story balcony. I droped to my knees as I saw my lifeless friend crucified before my very eyes. Rose and Tim came through the door and stoped when they saw me. Then, Rose followed my gaze up to Bryan. She cried out and droped to her knees.

Hatred filled me like never before. Tears ran down my face as I rose to my feet. It took every ounce of my control not to blur up to Bryan and rip the cross from the balcony. I turned and ran into the house and up the stairs. I ran into my room to find it covered in blood. One inch long blades were scattered across my room. Bryan was tortured, tortured just like the one......

It was 512, I was determined to have a normal life without religion. There was a priest who was determined to convert me. He came back day after day, confessing to me what the Lord had done for him. I tried to convince him to leave me be, but he wouldn't listen.

Two years before, I was tortured because of my beliefs. They tormented me day and night, demanding that I convert and repent for my ways. Thankfully a group of soldiers destroyed that place and set all of the prisoners free. They did not force me to convert, but they had caused me to lose all faith. Unfortunatly for this priest, he was sturring memories of my days in captivity.

One night a nightmare plagued me. I dreamed that the priest would come one day and decide to force me to convert. I woke in a cold sweat. I got up to take a walk, and found the priest on my front step. I still don't know what came over me, but I grabed the priest and threw him inside. I tortured him for three days before hanging him from a cross in my front yard to die. That night I tried to kill myself, but I didn't die. The villagers came the next day, and I ran. I ran from what I did, from who I was, and the monster I had become.

I came back to the present to find myself on my knees. Cain and Rose were both at my side. The police were there taking Bryan from the cross. The note wasn't the threat, but the warning. What he did to Bryan was the threat that I was to heed. This guy made one big mistake. He just made it personal.

THE HUNT IS ON

"PLEASE THINK ABOUT WHAT YOU'RE DOING!" CAIN begged.

"I have, Cain. This guy must die for what he has done," I answered.

"What about Rose?" Cain tried.

"She isn't safe while he lives. I'm doing this for her own good," I returned.

"Then let her decide what you should do next!" Cain snapped.

"Yes, Shade, let me decide," Rose added.

"I know you are scared and that is why I have to do this," I informed her.

"But this isn't for me is it?" Rose shot back.

"I won't let this madman near you," I answered.

"Shade, please, just stay with me," Rose tried.

"Shade, the council is conviening in two hours. Please come, after all you are just as in charge as me," Cain interjected.

"I need to find him and finish this," I told them.

"We will," Cain stated.

"Shade, don't do this alone. You are better than him, but doing this makes you just like him," Rose said through sobs.

"I am just like him. I am a Forsaken because, I killed a priest in the same fashion. I was tortured when I was young in a means to convert me. A few years later, a priest came day after day to convert me. One day I just snapped. I tortured him for two days, before hanging him on a cross. He did nothing wrong, but I killed him," I informed them.

"That was then. This is now. You aren't that man anymore. You are a man who values life, so please stay with me and work with Cain," Rose said grabbing onto me.

"I have four men ready to watch over Rose while we decide what to do," Cain added.

"Alright, let's finish this," I decided.

Cain and I got ready for the meeting while waiting for Cain's men to show up. Rose was down stairs trying to deal with the police. Cain's men finally showed up as the police started to leave. Steven was at the head of the pack. I smiled in greetings and shook his hand.

"Steven, you are in charge of security?" I asked.

"Who better?" Steven answered.

"Steven is the best at security of all the Forsaken. These four with him are to make sure he won't be overpowered," Cain added.

"Rose will be safe with me and this bunch. If we fail, it's because there were at least eight of them," Steven joked.

He nodded to the other three and they blurred out of sight. I nodded to Steven. I turned to see Rose wiping tears from her face. She gave me a hug and buried her face into my chest. I kissed her forehead. Cain put his hand on my shoulder to let me know that it was time to go. I nodded and took a step away from Rose. She didn't look up. I put my hand under her chin and lifted her face to look at me.

"I will protect you," I promised.

With that I kissed Rose. She closed her eyes and pushed into the kiss. I took a step back and blurred away with Cain. I watched Steven escort Rose back into the house from across town. Cain waited for me.

We made it to the council room just in time. Knome was trying to get everybody to calm down. Broad was just leaning against the wall relaxing. Skull was running around stopping anyone from leaving. Mathew was standing in Cain's spot trying to take the leadership role. Wolf actually started tying the others up.

"ENOUGH!" Cain exclaimed.

Everyone stopped what they were doing. Mathew jumped down to his spot. Within seconds everyone was standing infront of their doorway. Cain and I jumped to our spots to start the meeting.

"What is going on?" I asked as I scanned the room.

"There is a panic involving the knowledge of new Forsaken," Wolf explained breifly.

"If this is true, we can regain our numbers," a very short Forsaken called from the bottom of the chamber.

"Not if these undisclosed Forsaken are out to kill us," Knome piped up.

"We have no proof of that," the short one returned.

"One of them is trying to kill me, Morph," I shot at the short one.

"That sounds like a personal problem," Morph returned.

"If you don't shut your mouth, you'll be dead by the end of the day," I warned.

"Enough, Morph. I won't stop him from killing you and neither will the council," Cain informed him.

Morph's eyes went very wide. He bowed his head and took a step back. Murmurs spread across the council chamber. Cain was not one to tolerate fighting, but with this exception, everyone knew I meant business. I glared around the chamber until it was dead quiet. I took this as having everyones' full attention.

"I have been targeted by a new Forsaken, who has made it a piont to inform me that I have sined against him and will suffer for it. This leads me to believe he became a Forsaken to follow and destroy me. If there are others like him, they will likely have a simulair goal, and any of us could be their target. We stand to be erradicated by a group not unlike our own. We need to find the one that is after me, and get information on any others like him. That is our best option," I explained in full.

"Why don't we let you two fight it out and keep the winner?" Morph suggested.

"Did you not hear the part where any of us could be targets?" Skull snapped.

"There is no evidence to support that theory," a fat Forsaken said flatly.

"And there is none to say that we are perfectly safe. There are, however, reports of Forsaken being killed off. Now, Morph, Frank, unless the two of you know something we don't about that, we have to assume that the hidden Forsaken are behind it, and seek out this information. Does anyone other than Morph and Frank disagree?" Cain added.

There were a few murmurs amoung the other, but no one spoke up if they did disagree. Cain nodded to me. I smiled and returned the gester. We both leapt from our spot to the floor below. Wolf, Skull, Mathew, and Broad followed us. Within a few minutes the whole council was on the floor. We split into groups of four. Due to an odd number, Cain and I were partnered with Morph. He didn't seem too keen on this either.

Frank was stuck with Wolf which made me feel much better. We all headed to Mt. Gad, where we would start our search.

"Does everyone know their route?" I asked as I walked around the group.

"Yes," several of them said, Wolf being the loudest.

"Good, the new Forsaken should be within the fifty mile radius we have set up If he isn't, we will expand the search by twenty-five miles. Is everyone clear?" Cain double checked.

Everyone nodded. With that everyone blurred away, except Cain, Morph, and myself. We decided to be the base since we had fewer people. Morph didn't seem to mind but I did. I wanted to be the one to find this monster and make him pay. True, I would have my chance, but not the way I wanted it. I wanted to ripe his insides out, peice by peice. I had a list of things to do, and everyone of them would result in me killing this guy.

Neither Cain nor I trusted Morph after his actions in the council chamber earlier that day. We both kept a very close eye on him. Oddly, he didn't do anything. I mean, he sat perfectly still, as if he were a statue. If he were human this would have bothered us, but we didn't have to breathe, so we just figured he was being patient.

BETRAYAL

IT HAD ONLY BEEN A FEW MINUTES since the other council members left, but it felt like a lifetime. Something about Morph made me worry. Cain paced around as though he couldn't sit still. I was getting tempted to join him when something surprised both of us.

"How far do you think they have made it?" Morph asked completly out of the blue.

"I don't think anyone will return for at least another half an hour. Why?" Cain answered.

"Good, that gives us plenty of time," Morph said to himself.

"Time for what?" I asked with traces of suspicion in my voice.

Before anything else could be said, the ground swollowed Cain and Morph. Shackles wraped around my arms. They connected themselves to the ground restricting my movement to a ten foot radius. Then from the ground, a man came forth. He walked toward me without a word. It was the man we were looking for. He steped in close and swung. I swung around and kicked him in his gut, sending him back a few feet. He quickly recovered, but did not take a step toward me.

"It seems that even bound, you are still capable of stoping your own death," the figure stated.

"I can kill while wearing these shackles!" I exclaimed.

"Perhaps. Since I can't kill you now, I'll give you a history leason, as well as my name. I am called Relic. I have killed your accomplice in the crime you have commited against me and my family. Now that just leaves you before I can rest. Do you recall a small boomtown out west?" Relic started explaining.

"Um, Relic is it, do you know how many boomtowns there were in the west? I was in almost every one of them for a few days at the very least," I spat.

"I guess you don't remember destroying one of those towns either?" Rellic toyed.

"Two actually," I answered smoothly.

"Two? Well I was the soul surviver of one of those two towns. You and a Forsaken named Smite, locked everyone in the town hall and burned it down. Smite is dead. I killed him for his sins," Relic informed me.

"That's nice, but not your job. I remember your father. You look alot like him. He was the leader of a group of religious finatics who aimed to destroy all of the Forsaken. Survival instincts are hard to throw. Smite and I defended ourselves. Yes, we killed everyone so that no one would be coming after us. Nothing personal, just survival," I recalled.

"Don't speak of my father! You two missed one and now I've come to collect. I will kill you, very, very, soon," Relic snapped.

With that he was gone. It seemed as though the shackles were not his doing, because they still bound me to the earth. This could only mean one thing, Morph had betrayed us.

I fell through the earth before I knew anything was happening. When I regained my senses, I was bound in shackles. Morph was a few feet away, bound, the same as me. I looked around. We had been swollowed by the mountain. Morph walked toward me. He showed no sign of worry or fear. Something wasn't right with this guy.

"Any idea what happened?" Morph asked me as he approached.

"I got nothing," I answered as I turned to examine the wall behind me.

Without warning, I was hit in the head and sent flying across the cave. I began sliding so I rolled back onto my feet. I looked back to see Morph standing there unmoved, but he was no longer shackled as I was. How did he get unshackled? He was never shackled to begin with, but my shackles were still there. This was Morph's doing.

"Figure it out yet?" Morph asked me calmly.

"You've betrayed us," I growled.

"I was never with you. I'm a spy, always have been," Morph said with a delighted chuckle.

"What? How can that be?" I wondered outloud.

"It's true that there are more Forsaken that are younger than Shade, but they aren't the only ones out for blood. There is a whole organization of us, and now is the time we have been waiting for," Morph explained.

"And what's that?" I questioned.

"War with the Forsaken of this world. We want to exterminate all of you," Morph answered with a laugh.

"How many guys do you have? And what do you mean? Are there Forsaken among you who have been alive for more than two thousand years or something?" I inquired.

"Just two with that kind of lifespand. Everyone else is a thousand or younger," Morph informed me.

"And you think you can take us?" I returned with a smirk.

"Laugh it up, but we match your numbers, fool," Morph snarled.

"That won't be enough. We have centuries of experience on most of your comrades," I retorted.

"But now you are the only one older than the master. You are his reason for living. He will kill you," Morph spat.

"Doubt it," I countered as I destroyed the shackles.

"How did you?" Morph began.

"Lilith was only the second strongest Forsaken, physically at least. I, however, have no restrictions. You were dead the moment you hit me," I told him.

"We shall see," Morph smiled.

Morph launched himself at me. He came to a dead stop two feet in front of me. He couldn't move. He was stuck in mid-stride. A wicked grin crossed my face. Morph was only seconds away from death. He strained to move, even an inch, but it was pointless. I had him and it was time to finish this arguement.

I raised my hand to his head. I grabbed his face and squeezed. It only took a second for me to pull his head off. I threw it across the cave and looked for the best way out. It was right over where I fell at. I walked over to the spot and jumped.

The shackles vanished without warning. Cain had just killed Morph. Serves him right for betraying us. I would have to wait for Cain and the others to return, before trying to go after Relic. By the code made by the council, Relic wanted revenge on me, which made it my job to resolve it without the council's help. I would let them know as soon as they returned.

The ground shook a little. I looked at where Cain was before he fell. There was a huge hole, and standing next to it was a blood-stained Cain. He smiled at me as he examined the surroundings. He gave my a funny, puzzled look when he finished looking.

"I figured you were the target of that attack," Cain said calmly.

"I was. His name is Relic. I killed his family a long time ago. That makes this a personal dispute between the two of us. The council is no longer needed to resolve the matter," I informed him.

"You are half right. It's a declaration of war. Morph spilled before I killed him. We have an enemy, that could actually kill us," Cain explained to me.

This was a shock to me. I had heard the rumors, but to think that it makes Cain feel this way can only mean one thing. These rogues match our numbers at the very least. Panic rose in my chest. How many were going to come after Rose in an attempt to get to me. Panic was quickly replaced by anger. I had no intention of letting anyone harm Rose, ever.

"I need to go after Relic," I told Cain.

"I know. Go ahead. I'll inform the council of the recent events. We need to handle this quickly and quietly. Go see Rose before you go, ok?" Cain allowed.

I nodded in agreement. Cain smiled as I blurred away.

MEET ME

I ARRIVED AT THE HOUSE TO FIND all four of the security detail locked in battle. Steven was on the house steps. The others were fighting in the front yard. I didn't see Rose anywhere. I blurred over to the closet of the security team. He was on his back trying to stop a sword. I came up behind his attacker and took the sword from him. I rammed it through his chest and slashed it upward. The one I saved nodded and blurred toward one of the others while I threw the sword into another enemy's chest. He dropped to his knee as his opponent grabed his head and pulled it off. The one I just saved grabbed the other and held him for his friend to finish. I blurred over to Steven.

Steven was badly hurt. He looked as though he had been stabbed in the back. Reguardless of his wounds, Steven was holding his own. I ran up behind the final intruder. He jumped across the porch so his back wasn't to either of us. He glanced over to see the others in heaps on the ground. He hissed, realizing that he was alone against five.

"Give up, you're alone and out numbered. If you surrender, I promise to spare your life. What say you?" I offered.

"We will never surrender to you monsters. We exist to destroy your kind, and we will destroy all of you," the intruder spat.

"I'm afraid I can't let you leave, one way or the other," I warned.

"Try to take me," the intruder challenged.

I sent a surge of power at him. It sent him flying into the air across the yard. He landed on his head. Two of the security team blurred over to him. They grabed him before he could get any kind of footing. They pinned him down and waited for further instructions. I walked over to them, knowing that there was nothing the intruder could do.

"Chain him down so there is no way he could possibly kill himself," I ordered.

They nodded and pulled him up. The third security guard followed closely behind them. Steven limped over to me. He looked really bad, but he look disappointed. I had the feeling that he failed to stop Relic from getting Rose. I had to find her and kill him.

"Did he leave anything behind?" I asked without any hint of anger.

"I don't know. His friends kept me down here while he got her. I tried to stop him, but his friend got in the way long enough for him to stab me. I'm sor," Steven explained.

"Don't be sorry. You almost died. I could ask nothing more of any of you. You were out matched, nothing more. You need to get taken care of. I'll handle Relic myself," I informed him.

"Are you sure?" Steven asked a little wary of my intentions.

"This is a personal vendeta, as well as, a prelude to a war. We will need you at your best very soon. Trust me," I told him.

"I always have, even if it got me into trouble. Do me one favor and come back in one peice," Steven agreed.

"You know I will. I have to celebrate my honeymoon," I joked.

We both laughed as we headed into the house. Steven went into the livingroom to fix himself up. I started blurring around the house, looking for any clues as to where Relic may have taken Rose. It wasn't hard. He left a note on my blood-stained bed.

> Now that I have your attention, I have the woman you claim to love. If you don't meet me in the park in exactly one hour, I will kill her. I know she knows your secret, so I have no choice, but to issue a threat against her life. You must come alone and unarmed. We will fight to the death. If you win she will go home with you. If you lose, I will gladly take my own life. Either way, as long as you show up, you will have saved her life. One hour.
> Relic

Saving her seemed to be the easy part. Being able to stay with her till the day she died, that was becoming a problem. I knew I was going to save her, but what I had to figure out was how to survive. I know he had to of set this up to give him an edge in the fight. He may or may not know what I'm capable of, but I had to assume that he did. With this in mind and his performance on the mountain top, he was going to use weapons. Whether or not I would be given a weapon to fight with, was something I could only hope for. If he wanted terms, he would ask for a purely physical fight, which would limit me severly. I was skilled one way or the other, the only question was if I'm better than Relic.

Cain was suddenly behind me. He looked annoyed. He took a step forward. He looked over my shoulder and read the note. He hissed when he was done. Something was definately wrong.

"What is it?" I asked casually.

"The council over ruled me. They want Relic alive for information," Cain explained.

"No we don't. I captured one of his accomplices. We have him subdued for now. You and the council will be free to interigate him when ever you see fit. I will not let Relic live. If I should fall, he plans to take his own life. He would have his revenge and no more need to be what he is," I explained.

"We should let the council know so that they can release their decision. What kind of man becomes what he despises most to get revenge?" Cain wondered as he left the room.

"What kind indeed?" I whispered.

I turned and followed Cain down the stairs. Most of the council was on my front yard. We sent a few out to gather the rest. While we waited for their return, Cain and I checked on Steven. He had a closer call than he cared to addmit, but he would be fine. The last two council members arrived so we went out to discuss the new turn of events.

"Those of the council, we have captured one of the enemy. He is being held prisoner inside. Relic has issued a challenge to Shade. He wants a fight to the death. In order for Shade to ablige, he needs us to overrule the decision to spare Relic's life at all costs. What say you?" Cain explained.

"Is it nesasary to kill him, Shade?" Frank questioned.

"Careful, Frank. Morph was the only one besides you who spoke up for the enemy, and he turned out to be one of them," I warned.

"Yes, but logically, two informats are better than one, especailly if we have the one who was incharge," Frank stated calmly.

"I must agree, but this man won't allow us to take him alive, and our rules are very clear about challenges," I contested.

"Then the council shall decide," Frank said with a nod.

"Who agrees to overrule our previous decision to allow Relic to live?" Cain asked us all.

Almost everyone raised their hand. Only five didn't, and I knew that Cain was going to investigate them all. He nodded to me, giving me permission to go kill Relic. Then he preceeded to giving orders. He wanted all the remaining Forsaken here to prepare for a fight with these rogues. I knew that upon my return, there would be a war-council called to order. I also knew that Cain wanted all the best warriors to be part of it, including me.

As I walked through the crowd of my fellow Forsaken, they shoke my hand and wished me luck. They all knew what path we were on, and that we would all have to pull together to face this threat. They knew that if we were going to keep on living, that they would need everyone, especailly me and Cain.

DISCLOSURE

I MADE IT TO THE PARK IN no time. Unfortunately, it was crowded. It seemed that Relic didn't trust me to leave the others behind. There was no way he'd start a fight with so many innocents nearby. I didn't know him, but I knew he wanted to save lives and take vengance. To fight here with so many witnesses, is to condemn them all to death. No he wanted to release Rose here, and take the fight somewhere else.

I walked around looking for any sign of them. I had walked the whole length of the park before I saw them. Relic was standing behind Rose over by the woods. Rose looked scared, but safe. Relic motioned for me to come over. I nodded and approached them. He smiled and whispered to Rose as I got close. She bowed her head and began crying. I wasn't sure what he said to her, but I would make sure he regreted it. I stoped a few feet away from them.

"I, Shade, have accepted your challenge for a fight to the death. You may release Rose now and face me where ever you see fit," I declared.

""Very good. Rose, dear, run on home to your parents. I'm sure there are too many Forsaken at Shade's house for it to be safe," Relic said with a pleased smile.

"Rose, Cain is waiting for you," I told her.

"Did Steven or any of the others die?" Rose asked me as she walked toward me.

"No, they are all just fine. I'll be home shortly," I answered.

"No you won't. And as I said, it isn't safe for her at your house," Relic sneered.

"Safer there than at her parents," I snapped.

Rose ran into my arms, crying. I kissed her forehead and hugged her tight. She looked up at me and mouthed something. I kissed her lips and let her go. She lingered for a moment, before deciding it was best to go and leave the fighting to me. I didn't even look after her as she ran from me.

"Follow me," Relic ordered.

I nodded. Relic turned into the woods. I blurred after him. We ran for almost an hour, before coming to a stop in the middle of a peaceful forest. I soaked in the beauty of our surroundings as we came to a stop. It was one of the most beautiful places to die. Why did he pick a place like this for someone he marked as a monster? I wondered this as he turned to face me.

"Amazing, isn't it?" Relic asked.

"Truely," I replied.

"This will be my resting place, one way or the other," Relic answered my unasked question.

"I will make sure you get a proper burial if I win," I vowed.

"Why? Why would a monster like yourself, care to do that for me?" Relic asked.

"Forsaken are not without honor. Not all of us, at least. I addmit to my youthful mistakes, and will gladly pay for each and every one of them," I informed him.

"Good, cause I plan on making sure of that," Relic sneered.

"And what of the sins you have commited?" I inquired.

"I will pay for them in death," Relic answered quickly as though he expected me to ask.

"As will I, so why do you believe that it is your place to punish me?" I demanded.

"It isn't. This is revenge. I know it isn't right, but in this world, what is?" Relic pointed out.

"How right you are. I have to ask, what did you tell Rose as I approached the two of you?" I asked.

"That it was a shame to kill you and leave her all alone. I wish I had found what the two of you have, but I was too busy looking for you and Smite. Now it is almost over. What did Rose tell you when she was in your arms?" Relic asked with a look of curiosity on his face.

"That you are simply a victim who lost his way," I answered.

"That's nice. She understood everything I said.

"She is a wonderful person. I don't know why I was matched with her. If only she had been born in my time, maybe then neither of us would be here now," I thought outloud.

"I think this moment was innevitable. I think we were destined to fight to the death," Relic mused.

"I hate destiny. It's so cruel and without purpose," I spat.

"Not always without purpose, but yes, it is cruel," Relic replied as he drew two swords."I think I should tell you about the Avengers. We are just like you Forsaken. We do have one difference. We live to kill your kind. We are the equalizer placed on this planet to respond to your kind. Our leader was once three men. They had no name, but were called Trinity. Now only one remains. He is our leader. If you want to stop us, he has to be your target," Relic informed me.

"Why are you telling me this?" I puzzled.

"Because they are becoming just like your kind. They don't see humans and Forsaken. They kill any who get in their way. They are becoming monsters," Relic explained.

"They aren't the only ones. The Forsaken went into hiding, because when discovered, the humans went mad. They did whatever it took to kill us. They became monsters through fear of us. The Avengers are the same, but they found a way to become us in the process. Do you know how hard it is to become a Forsaken now? People sin almost every minute of every day, but they don't become us. The people of this time, they are lost, and there will come a day when they will be the monsters and the Forsaken will be the few good people left," I lectured.

"That may come to pass, but only if the Forsaken survive the onslaught," Relic spat.

"We have centuries of experience on all of you. It is unfortunate that we must be enemies. It would have been good to have known you on better terms," I told him.

"I agree, we may have been friends," Relic nodded.

"But now, we both have vengence to take care of," I stated.

"And who do you have to avenge?" Relic demanded.

"My best friend, Bryan, the man you tortured and crucified!" I declared.

"He attacked me. I defended myself and used the corpse to send a message," Relic tried to justify.

"He was a priest hellbent on saving my soul. You killed one of the few good humans left in this world, and for that, I must kill you," I explained.

"You killed hundreds. For that, I will kill you. Here is a sword for you to use. We will fight on fair ground, as equals," Relic said as he threw the sword to me.

"Yes we shall," I agreed while catching the sword in my right hand.

A breeze picked up above us. We both took stances with swords in hand. We were waiting for God to start the fight.

ALL GOOD MEN
MUST DIE SOME DAY

THE BREEZE STOPED AND THE FIGHT BEGAN. Relic and I charged each other. Our swords clashed for only a second before we pulled back and launched another attack. I blocked his swing with my left arm. He brushed my blade to the side as I pushed it toward his face. He planted his palm in my chest knocking me back several yards. I jumped to the side to dodge his downward thrust. I charged back in with my sword in the lead, but Relic managed to step back before I stabbed him. He swung low trying to catch me in the stomach. I jumped over his blade and rolled into a stance. Relic stepped back into his stance.

"You're impressive," Relic commented.

"You too for a young one," I returned.

"This has been my passion for over a hundred years. I think I've picked up a few tricks along the way," Relic smerked.

"Don't get cocky. That'll get you killed," I retorted.

"Only if I let it go to my head," Relic pointed out.

I nodded and we charged each other again. This time I stopped short and waited for his sword to pass. It didn't. When it was pointed at my head, Relic stepped forward. I narrowly stepped out of the way. He stopped and brought the sword down at me. I pushed it beneath me and swung at his head. Relic bent backward to avoid it. I landed with a back swing hoping to catch him coming back up, but he kicked himself into a backflip, kicking my arm away. My sword flew behind me. I blurred over to where it would land.

Just before it was in my reach, Relic was on me. He thrust his sword into my side. I caught my sword and swung down. I heard clothe rip as he jumped back, removing his sword from my side. I wiped my blade with my hand. There was a little blood on the end of it. Relic charged me with a back stroke, but I blocked it and pushed it upward. I stepped forward and rammed my fist into his gut, lifting him over my head. I let him fly over me and hit the ground a few feet away. I ran over and swung low in an attempt to take his head off, but he rolled out of the way.

"It seems that I picked my fight well, however, it seems you are a fighter in any aspect of the word," Relic commended.

"The term is warrior. Yes, I am and will always be a warrior. That is why I will kill you," I addmitted.

"Good. I didn't want this to be easy. The best things in life, are the things hardest to earn," Relic laughed.

"But you aren't alive anymore. You died when you became what you are," I spat.

"I'm no different than you," Relic snarled.

"You live for revenge. That isn't my goal in life. I still live to the fullest. You threw everything away for revenge. You became a hollow creature for nothing. You are pathetic," I snapped.

"I'll show you pathetic," Relic snarled as he mounted another charge.

Relic came at me with a downward stroke. It was powerful, but left him very vulnerable. I stepped to the side and jabbed my sword at him. I started into his upper side, but he stepped away and swung at me. I leaned away from his attack and swung over my head to hit him. He shouldered his blade to block my strike. I took a step back to look for another openning, but he took a low swing at me, forcing me to jump back. Relic leapt toward me and caught me in the face with a left hook. I stumbled to the ground, but rolled back to my feet. He tried for another shot, but I caught him and knocked his sword out of his hand. He hit me with another hook, forcing me to release him.

Relic quickly moved to reclaim his weapon. I ran after him with a down swing. Relic managed to get his sword, but I managed to slice open his shoulder. Relic rolled to avoid any further damage. He got back to his feet and swung to make me abandon my charge. I jumped back and regained my stance. Relic did the same.

"Fiving up so soon?" Relic mocked.

"Ha. You seem to be getting worse," I retorted.

"Still better than you," Relic snarled.

"Not for much longer," I chuckled.

We charged each other again. This time when we clashed, we held that position. We glared at each other, trying to guess what the other was about to do. Without warning, Relic rammed his knee into my side. My feet came off the ground for just a second. As soon as my feet hit the ground, I returned the favor by ramming my knee into his gut. His guard shifted for just a second, but it was enough time for me to act. I grabbed his arm and threw him over my shoulder.

Relic landed at the edge of the tree line. He got up as quickly as possible, but he was showing signs of weakening. Unfortunatly, I was begining to feel weak. I had to finish this quickly. Relic got ready to charge. I prepared to intercept him. Relic smiled an evil grin. He knew it was almost over, but he seemed happy, even though it looked as though he was going to be the one to die. Did he have some trick up his sleeve?

"You are much stronger than Smite was. He died after the second swing of my sword. Hehe, I have longed for a fight that would bring me this feeling. Thank you, Shade," Relic said whole-heartedly.

"It has been a pleasure, Relic. Now it's over," I said with a smile.

We charged each other for one last time. We clashed swords again. This time I grabbed his hands and swung my fist around, punching him in the face. Relic swept his left foot under me. I fell back, but I rolled backward and pushed myself into the air. I landed on my feet as Relic came after me. As he swung at me, I grabbed his sword by the flat side and punched my sword through Relic's chest. I ripped it to the side, openning up his chest. I stepped behind him and put my sword to his throat.

"Goodbye, Relic," I whispered into his ear.

I pulled the sword across his throat. I stepped back and slashed backward. Relic fell backward and hit the ground. Blood poured from his neck, pooling around his body. I stabbed my sword into the ground just above Relic's head. I bowed my head to pay my respects, then turned and walked away. I didn't blur until I hit the treeline. I never looked back at the mess I left behind.

REGRET

I MADE IT HOME JUST AS ROSE made it to the top step. Cain was standing there to greet her. The council was still in my front yard waiting for my return. They began cheering as I approached. Rose stopped and turned to face me. A smile filled her face as tears rolled down her cheeks. She ran off the porch to meet me, but I couldn't wait. I blurred to her and hugged her tight. She hugged me back. She cried uncontrollably as she buried herself into my chest. The cheering died away. I looked up at Cain, he nodded in congratulations.

Steven walked onto the porch and stood next to Cain. I nodded to him. A smile stretched across his face as he watched Rose in my arms. I picked Rose up and walked her back to the house. The council closed the gap behind us. I nodded to each of them as I walked. They all smiled in return.

It's funny how we were the ones who commited the worst crimes of all time, yet, we had come together to defend ourselves. As I told Relic, one day we would be the ones with morals, and the humans.... well they would be the ones with a murderous intent. Watching the other members of the council gather around to make sure that Rose and I were alright, it was all the proof I needed.

"Please tell me that you won't put me through that again?" Rose hoped.

"Unfortunatly, there is a war coming. It will be the first of many to come. All of us, will have to stick together to save our way of life. I'm sorry, but because of what I am, this will never end," I apologized.

"Then I have no choice," Rose said. I bowed my head believing that she was about to leave me. "I have to stay by your side through all of it. I love you, Shade, and I will never leave you. I promise."

"I love you so much," I told her. I smiled and kissed her as we reached the top step of our home. I set her down and shook Cain's hand. We turned to face the council.

I froze in fear. Cain tensed up next to me. Rose screamed as she saw him standing behind the council. Everyone turned to see what we were looking at. Relic stood there at the back of the crowd, staring straight at me. He looked mad, but defeated at the same time. He took a step forward. Several council members in the back stepped toward him.

"No this was my fight. I have to finish it," I called.

"You promised to bury me, if I lost. You didn't bury me," Relic spat with blood pouring from his mouth.

"This is why you followed me. Well I never break my promises, so now you die. I will return your body to that place and bury you by myself," I declared.

"No, I will help you bury him. Relic has proven to be a great warrior, and I wish to help give him a proper burial," Cain insisted.

I nodded to Cain, who nodded back. The council began whispering among itself. I turned to Relic, who nodded in agreement. I launched myself across my yard and grabbed Relic. He stabbed in the side with his sword, but I ignored the pain. I grabbed his head and pulled it off. Cain blurred next to me and grabbed Relic's body and waited for me to lead the way. I nodded to him and blurred back through the park, on to the clearing in the woods.

Cain and I set the two peices of Relic's body at the edge of the clearing. Then, Cain and I started digging a hole with our bare hands. We made it twelve feet deep, so that no one would bother Relic's body while he slept. Cain and I set his body and head in the grave and began replacing the dirt. When we were finished we both took a seat at the edge of the clearing.

"Do you think this is what he wanted?" Cain asked me.

"This and me dead," I replied.

"Not Relic, God," Cain corrected.

"I don't know. What I do know is that at the rate things are going, most of us won't live to see the next century. I can only hope for the best," I answered.

"Well said, sounds a bit like a human though," Cain pointed out.

"Well my friend, I think that the humans will be the monsters before it's all said and done," I informed him.

"I believe you're right. I think the only ones that will accept us are our soul mates. I regret that we have done so much harm that a very powerful enemy has emerged to try and kill us all," Cain agreed.

"As we always believed, it's us against the world. My only regret is that Rose has to bare this burden with me," I said while staring into the sky.

Cain just looked down. He was lost in thought. I knew it was the future that plagued him, but neither of us knew what the future held for us, just that it was going to be hard, and that we, the Forsaken, would be united to face it all. With this in mind, I patted Cain's back and stood up. He followed my lead.

"It's time to get back. We have alot to do. Plus, I have a wife to go home to. Let's go, Cain," I said. Cain nodded in agreement.

He looked at me and smiled. He figured out what he was trying to wrap his mind around, and I was sure that he would tell me when the time was right, till then, I wasn't worried. We took one last look at Relic's grave, before blurring back home.

WAR OF THE CURSED

TOWN GOSSIP

IT HAD BEEN A FEW MONTHS SINCE I killed Relic. The council members used my house as one of many bases we had scattered across the world. The council chamber was the only other base in the United States. Cain was very rarely found there though. He spent most of his time at my house with me and Rose. This meant that Steven was either here or on mission, so he managed to do most of the house work.

I had managed to limit suspicion of something strange going on at my house, by requesting that any Forsaken who choose or needed to take shelter at my home, used cars or simuliar means to get here. Cain was the only one who never did this, but he bought a car for when he decided to go into town. This suited me fine, unfortunatly, it didn't give me much alone time with Rose. Don't worry, I took every chance I got to be with her.

As far as the Avengers were concerned, we hadn't been able to find as much information as we wanted. The one we captured in Relic's attack proved to be very stupid. He didn't know much at all. This told me that they had lackies who weren't part of the inner circle. Wolf disposed of the prisoner once we determined that he was of no further use to us. Other than that, we managed to find one of their hideouts. It was more like a safehouse they set up for their own to hide in case of emergencies. There were only two of them in there when we raided it.

I still couldn't figure out how they knew so much about us, but we could barely find any information on them. It seemed as though Morph had given them alot. We were at a disadvantage that could cost us our lives.

"Skull, have you seen Rose?" I called across the kitchen.

"Yea, she went to the store. Said yall didn't have enough food for everyone that was here. Steven went with her to help carry them," Skull called back.

It was breakfast and we had six guests including Skull. Cain was up in his room, undoubtably still asleep. I grabbed two peices of toast and got out of the way. True, we don't have to eat, but we love the taste, so we eat what we love. I managed to get out of the kitchen alive. I went and sat in the livingroom to wait for Rose to get back. I turned the tv on to watch the news.

There seemed to have been a murder in New York. They were giving the details of the slaughter as they wheeled the body out of the alley. They said his throat was slit and that his chest was ripped open. That would be enough to kill any Forsaken I knew. The reporter said that the police wouldn't show us the body, but she had managed to get his name and had a picture ready. When the picture came on the screen, I crushed the remote.

It was Echo. Cain and I sent him to investigate clubs in New York to see if he found anything. We last heard from him three days ago. He said he had heard rumors of a cult trying to recruit people with the promise of immortality. I asked him to find and tail one of the recruiters to see if it was the enemy. Evidently, he was on the right path, but was dicovered. This gave me a new assignment. I got up and turned the tv off as I heard a car pull up.

I walked out to greet Rose and Steven. They had a car full of groceries so I called for the others to come help. We could only put so many bags in each hand before running out of room. We got everything inside and put up. I kissed Rose on the head and told her to get something to eat while I talked to Cain. She kissed my lips and grabbed the eggs. I smiled as I looked after her.

Rose was adjusting to this life rather well. She was always trying to stay busy so Cain and I could take care of business. She was my perfect match. She looked over at me as she started her eggs and stuck her tongue out at me. I returned the favor and started toward Cain's room.

I knocked on the door when I got to the top of the stairs.

"Enter," Cain called.

I entered the room and looked around. It looked as though he had been at it all night again. Cain was becoming obsessed with finding these Avengers. He did however look as though he had already taken a shower, as a matter of fact, he looked like he was going on a trip.

"Going some where?" I asked casually.

"New York," Cain answered without looking up.

"So you're one step ahead of me?" I inquired.

"I got the call last night. Echo said he found them. He told me what he knew and said he was going to keep an eye on them until I got there," Cain informed me.

"Cain, they found Echo's body this morning. He was discovered and killed," I informed Cain.

"Damnit, I'm too late. I have to go now," Cain hissed.

"I'll grab some things," I agreed.

"No, Shade, you stay here with Rose," Cain insisted.

"Cain, just because I'm married doesn't mean you can bench me. I'm going because you need someone to have your back on a mission like this," I explained.

"Wolf is meeting me there," Cain tried.

"Do you honestly think that is going to keep me from going?" I asked him with a wicked grin on my face.

"I had hoped," Cain admitted.

"To no aveil, my friend," I stated still smiling.

Cain nodded as I turned to go pack. When I was done, I found him waiting in the livingroom with Rose. She smiled weakly at me as I came into veiw. I set my bag down and held out my arms. She rushed into them and grabbed onto me. I hugged her and kissed her forhead.

"It seems that Rose has something she needs to tell you before we go," Cain said as he stood and walked out of the room.

"What is it, dear?" I asked with a puzzled expression on my face.

"There rumors flying around town about all of our guests. People think that you are up to something," Rose informed me.

"Small town gossip no doubt," I murmured.

"They think that you are trying to get an army ready to fight the government," Rose whispered.

I began laughing hesterically. Rose took a step back and scolded me. I settled down and looked at her as seriously as I could after that rediculous idea. I pulled her back into my arms and held her tight. She relaxed and snuggled into my chest.

"They couldn't prove that in a million years. Ok? Now, Steven knows what to do as far as the Forsaken go. You just worry about you. I love you," I assured her.

"I love you too," Rose replied.

I kissed her one last time before letting her go. I took a step back and grabbed my bag. Rose took a step forward and kissed me again. I hugged her one last time before walking out the door to join Cain for what was sure to be a long ride to New York.

THE BIG APPLE

THE PLANE RIDE WAS TERRIBLE. EVEN THOUGH we were flying first-class, we still had kids making all kinds of noise. The flight attendant spilled drinks on me once and Cain twice. She wouldn't even take her eyes off of either of us. It was annoying, especailly after she asked about my ring. When she found out I had a wife who was at home, she commented that my wife didn't have to know. Cain laughed then asked her to leave us alone so we could sleep. We pretended to sleep for an hour before the plane landed.

It didn't get any better when we got off the plane. I couldn't get a taxi. Cain tried and failed too. We ended up walking to the nearest hotel just to find out that they had no open rooms. The next hotel wanted us to make reservations. Finally, we found a building for sale. It looked like an old office building. Cain bought it so we had some place to stay while we were in town. We got settled in just before dark.

"What do we do first?" I wondered outloud.

"Nothing until Wolf gets here," Cain answered.

"When and where is he suppose to meet us?" I inquired.

"He said he would find me," Cain replied.

"And I have. Why didn't you two check into a hotel?" Wolf asked as he walked in the door.

"All the hotels we came to didn't have any opennings," I answered.

"Should've called ahead," Wolf mocked.

"We were in a bit of a rush," Cain stated.

"So where is Echo?" Wolf asked as he scoped out the place.

"I came because I saw Echo's dead body on the television. They discovered him," I explained.

Wolf bowed his head and nodded. Wolf was the one who recruited Echo for these kind of missions. Next to Wolf, Echo was the best tracker amoung the Forsaken. I knew that Wolf had to feel responsible for Echo's death, but it wasn't true. We all chose to do this and risk it all along the way.

"So when do we start?" Wolf asked.

"Right now," Cain replied. "We'll hit up the last couple of clubs Echo reported going to. This will put us within three days of his discovery."

"Unless they changed their routine due to a breach," Wolf added.

"Very possible," I agreed.

"Then where do we begin?" Cain wondered outloud.

"Might I make a suggestion? Why don't we pick up where Echo left off, just in case the Avengers are over confident. If we find nothing, then we split up to cover as much ground tommorow night," I offered.

"Sounds like a plan. Cain?" Wolf agreed.

"Let's do this," Cain responded with a grin.

Wolf and I nodded at Cain's response. We all got ready to go to a club, which involved very expensive, popular clothes, and a couple thousand dollars a peice. Wolf wasn't big on fancy clothes so Cain let him borrow some of his. As for the money, we were all very old and had plenty of time to save money, so it wasn't a problem. We met at the door when we finished getting ready. Cain and I looked Wolf over to make sure he didn't mess something up.

"I have worn these type of clothes before. I was at your wedding, remember," Wolf griped.

"You could of gotten help for all we knew," I retorted.

"I didn't even know you were there," Cain addmitted.

"Great friends you two are," Wolf murmured.

We all walked out the door and this time, thanks to Wolf, we got a cab. They dropped us off infront of the first club Echo had named. Wolf looked at me for some hint. I honestly didn't know. We both turned to Cain who just laughed at us. He seemed to know what kind of club this was, but didn't seem keen on telling us. I guess he wanted to see us squirm.

We walked up to the bouncer, who pointed to the end of the line. Cain held up a small roll of money. The bouncer took it and let us in. Wolf and I examined our surroundings as we walked to the bar. Cain went straight to the dance floor. He wanted to have a little fun while he was here, I assumed. Wolf and I got some drinks while we scoped out the place.

"There were beams of lights flashing all over the place. Each beam was a different color. We seemed to be a little over dressed for this club. We saw alot of the dancers wearing very odd looking clothes. Wolf was the one who pointed out the music to me. It didn't really sound like instruments so much as one of those keyboards with the different sounds on it. There wasn't even any singing. We still hadn't quite figured out what we had gotten ourselves into when Cain came over to the bar.

"It's a techno club," Cain smiled.

"Honestly, I have no idea what that is," I informed him. Wolf nodded to say he was with me.

"It's a little hard to explain. Seen anything outside of your surroundings yet?" Cain inquired.

"Nope," Wolf answered before I could.

"There is a recruiter in the corner. He hasn't noticed yall, but we do need to leave and check the other clubs," Cain informed us. We both nodded and followed him to the door.

Once out of the club, we began walking down the street. The other club was two blocks down. This time I had my money ready, just in case. There was no line, so we didn't have much trouble out of the bouncer. We walked into what had to be a club for rockers. Wolf and I both loosened up. This time Wolf was the one who went to the dance floor, which was more of a mosh pit. Cain and I took a seat at the bar and ordered two drinks.

"This is interesting," I commented.

Cain looked at me with a bit of surprise on his face. I just smiled at him as the bartender gave us our drinks.

"Did I miss something?" Cain asked with curiousity in his voice.

"The recruiter is about ten feet from Wolf," I answered with a smirk.

"Both clubs?" Cain whispered with a hint of irritation.

"How many clubs did Echo tell you?" I asked.

"Two more," Cain replied without looking up. He seemed deep in thought.

"How are we going to play this then?" I asked trying to break Cain out of his trance.

"Your plan will do fine," Cain answered looking at me breifly.

I was a bit concerned with Cain's behavior. It was very odd for him to seem so bothered. Wolf made his way over to us. He had some how managed to save his shirt from the horde of girls trying to use the mosh pit as an excuse to rip it off. He sat down behind Cain and looked back at the mosh pit. I was sure he was watching the recruiter, who was making her way to the edge of the mosh pit herself.

"Where to now?" Wolf asked.

"Three blocks over," Cain said as he finally broke out of his trance.

We all got up and left the club. Wolf took one last look into the mosh pit, but I had the feeling that the mosh pit wasn't the center of his attention. The bouncer nodded to us as we walked by him. We crossed the street and started toward the next club. When we got to it, none of us even tried to walk in. It was a gay bar for guys. Wolf and I both looked at Cain for directions to the next club.

"Too bad Mathew isn't here," Cain commented.

"Wait. Mathew's gay?" Wolf asked.

"Yup, I'm one of the few who knows. Why do you seem so surprised?" Cain stated.

"Cause I've been staying with him," Wolf said with some discust.

"He won't mess with you," I informed him. "You aren't his type."

"I guess this is the bar we won't investigate," Cain concluded.

"Then let's get a move on. We don't have forever to do this," I joked.

PAST FRIENDS

CAIN STARTED BACK ACROSS THE STREET. WOLF and I followed his lead. We walked almost six blocks, before seeing a line of about twenty people. They all looked like they had a good bit of money, which meant we weren't just going to walk to the front of the line like before. Judging by just the people in the line alone, I would be assigned this club for my stack out. We finally made it to the front of the line. At least half of the people in the line had been turned away, so we were a little worried.

"Names," the bouncer demanded.

"I'm sure we aren't on that list," Cain told him.

"Then you can't get in," the bouncer told us and pointed to the street.

"How do we get on the list?" Wolf asked.

"The owner has to put your name on there," he answered.

"And who is the owner?" Wolf asked another question.

"Jacob Vanholt," the bouncer replied. He looked at us with a bit of aggrivation.

"I know Jacob," I piped up.

The bouncer looked at me and snorted. He didn't believe me in the slightest, but I really did know Jacob. I gave him his first job at my vineyard in California.

"We will see about that. Name," the bouncer challenged.

"Theodore Hadow," I answered.

The bouncer put his hand to his ear and said something. He was wearing one of those two way radios. He nodded as someone gave him a reply. He put his finger up telling us to wait just a minute. As promised, he got another reply after a minute. He nodded as he was told what to do.

"Well, Mr. Hadow, it seems that the boss does know you. As a matter of fact, he would like for you to go to his office while your friends enjoy the club," the bouncer informed us.

We nodded. Cain and Wolf followed me in as the bouncer openned the door for us. A security guard met us at the door and offered to show me to Jacob's office. I accepted and told the other two to have fun. I followed the guard up a set of stairs. He openned a door and waved me into it. I nodded and walked in.

"I knew it!" a man exclaimed as I walked through the door. "You haven't aged in fifteen years."

"You were one of the three people I trusted most. So I told you my secret a long time ago, Jacob," I smiled.

"That you did, but you taught me so much more. It's because of you that I managed to open this club. You are welcome here any time, Shade," Jacob agreed.

"Thank you. I do have some business to attend to here in your club," I started to explain.

"You mean the disappearances?" Jacob inquired.

"What do you know of them?" I persisted.

"I know I'm not the only club with the problem. It's ussually one a night. And I have one guest, who never fails to show up, but can't be found to talk to the cops," Jacob told me.

"Are these windows one sided?" I asked as I pointed to them.

"Trick mirrors. That's him in the trench coat," Jacob pointed out.

"How does he get in?" I continued the questions.

"I don't know that, or how he gets out," Jacob replied before taking a sip of his drink.

"I take it you don't know much about him," I guessed.

"Afraid not. What am I unknowingly involved in?" Jacob inquired.

"My kind now has an enemy. They call themselves the Avengers. They are just like us,but want to kill us for our sins. I think they are taking recruits from your club, as well as three others. They are trying to start a war that will run over into the open world," i explained.

"So your two friends are fellow Forsaken. I'll put you on the list as long as you need to be on it. Helping you helps me, but further more, I still remember what happened to Jack when I told him. We can't let this become human knowledge. After what happened to him, I know that much for sure. I'll put a plus two on the list for you. The three of you can use my office for surveillance," Jacob was explaining.

"It's best if the others don't know that you know. They wouldn't understand. Besides, they have their own mission here," I interupted him.

"Alright. So what's this I hear about you being married?" Jacob demanded.

"It is a bond that can't be broken. I don't know how else to explain it. She loves me back. I can only assume that she is my soulmate," I answered him as I held my hand up to show him my wedding ban. I never took my eyes off of the recruiter. I was memorizing his face, posture, form, and the way he moved. I had to be able to find him quickly every night until it was time to move.

It was two in the morning so I bid Jacob a good night, which he returned, and went down to the others. We all left and went back to the office to discuss our plan. We all wanted showers, but Cain got there first, so we had to wait for the breifing. Wolf and I sat in the main room talking as we waited.

"It seems like only yesterday, that I was training Echo. He was one of my oldest friends. And one of the closest I had. You and Cain are the only other two that I can really rely on," Wolf spoke as he stared off into space.

"We will get the guy that killed him. I promise," I told him as Cain came back into the room.

Wolf blurred across the room before I realized that the bathroom was open. I sighed in defeat as Cain went over to his bags. I had a feeling that things were changing in this world around us, and that we would make it or break it. One way or another, it seemed that we had a role to play in the world that we tried so hard to remove ourselves from. It was coming, and we were going to be the ones to end it. What that meant, I did not know, but I didn't like it.

It felt like Wolf was in the shower forever. Then I realized he had been, because the sun was up. How I knew that was a mystery even to me. In this monster city, I couldn't see the sun through the buildings. It reminded me of why I chose to live in small towns. I loved the sun too much to only see it for a few hours a day. My cell phone started ringing. It was Rose. She called to check on me and tell me that she missed me. I told her I missed her too and that at this rate we may be home within the week. She sounded overjoyed, but unconvinced at the same time. Wolf finally walked out of the bathroom so I told Rose I had to take a shower and that I would call her back later in the day. She made me promise before getting off the phone.

I took this chance to jump in the shower. I sat down and let the water run over me. It was so relaxing that I almost lost focus on the world around me. No wonder it took Wolf so long to get out. The water refreshed me, but not as much as Rose does every time I hold her in my arms. I missed her smell, her warmth, her soft skin, her gentle eyes, and I hadn't even been gone two days yet. Being in love is hard for a Forsaken, who has to keep on the offense all the time. Maybe one day, for a few years at least, Rose and I would be able to just enjoy our lives together. That was all I wished for in this world, time with her.

THE CLUB WATCH

W HEN I GOT OUT OF THE SHOWER, Cain and Wolf were waiting on me. They looked as though they had been talking while I was in there. I looked at the time. It was four in the afternoon. I walked over to where they were sitting so we could discuss the plan.

"Bout time," Wolf laughed.

"Look who's talking," I retorted.

"Well, now that we all feel better, let's get down to business. We have three clubs to watch. Each of us is better suited in a different club. I'll take the techno club. Wolf, take the rocker club. Shade, take the fancy club," Cain decided.

A smile crawled across Wolf's face. I gave him a go to hell look because I figured it was meant to mock me. Wolf acted like he didn't know why I was mad, but he let the smile drop. Cain seemed to be waiting for us to give him our attention again. We both looked at him so he would continue.

"We leave just before dark. Actually, I think Shade should leave an hour before dark. After all his target is a good bit further than ours," Cain thought outloud.

"I can make it there just fine," I pointed out to him.

"If you say so. Anyway, tomorrow we will meet back here and discuss what we saw. That way we know what we are up against. Then, if we feel it is safe, we take them down, or we follow them to their hideout," Cain explained.

"Their hideout is below ground, most likely in the sewer system. I smelled it on the girl in the mosh pit," Wolf added.

"I don't think that they are turning everyone they take," I offered.

"What do you mean?" Cain asked.

"If they were turning everyone they took, they would have two to three times the man power we do. They would have attacked by now. They probably seperate them into two categories. They have those who will turn, and those who won't. The ones in the fancy club as you put it, are the easiest to be angry at. Lots of money, they get what they want. They have a great life. Take a homeless man and tell him to kill that person so that he can have a good life that would never end, my guess is that he won't hesitate," I explained.

"Very likely, but it is just as likely that the rich are offered immortallity for taking a life. There are few who can resist the pull of immortallity. I've seen it before, haven't you, Shade?" Cain pointed out.

"Yes, a long time ago. A man named Jack discovered my secret. He went after me, alone, because he wanted to be just like me. He wanted my power and my life," I recalled.

"That's why we can't let the humans discover us?" Wolf asked now understanding the rules of silence.

"Yes, it is," Cain answered.

"So we have our assignments. Next is to find out anything we can about the enemy, and report constantly to ensure that the rest know what we do," I established.

"Yes, If we are lucky, we may survive this mission to fight in the war," Cain added. Wolf and I nodded in agreement.

I called Rose at six, just as I promised. She was so sad without me, and wished that I would be home soon. I agreed and let her know just how much I missed her. It made her happy to know how much she meant to me. I don't think she would ever understand it, but I was glad she tried. We were on the phone for about half an hour before I decided that I needed to get back to business. We said our farwells and hung up the phone.

As the sun began to set almost an hour later, Wolf called us another cab. I promised to pay the bill since I had to go further than they did. They accepted my offer and got out without a word as we got to each of their stops. Finally, I was at my destination. I paid the driver and then got out. I started toward the back of the line, the bouncer flagged me down.

"Did I do something?" I asked.

"No, Mr. Hadow. You don't have to wait in line. Boss's orders," the bouncer answered.

"That sure helps," I smiled as I walked in.

I walked through the crowd and got a drink at the bar. I wanted a feel for the place, before I started my watch. When the bartender gave me my drink, a girl smiled from down the bar. I returned the smile and walked around the edge of the club until I reached the stairs. I preceeded up them and knocked on Jacob's office door.

"Come in, Shade," Jacob called.

"Cameras, I take it," I guessed as I walked through the door.

"Some of the best," Jacob replied. "I could have had a drink brought to you."

"I took the oppritunity to get a feel for your place. It'll help me incase of a problem," I informed him. Jacob met me at the window to watch our target.

"He left without taking anyone last night, almost as if he knew he was being watched," Jacob informed me.

"Not unlikely. We have a great many abilities, that no human could comprehend," I assumed.

"I don't doubt that for one minute. After all, I saw what happened when Jack confronted you," Jacob recalled.

"Yes, what you saw was only a portion of what I am capable of. I have only had to use my full power twice in my life. I didn't have a choice, and my opponent, didn't live for much longer," I explained without going into much detail.

"Sounds like you don't want it, but you use it to do what you must. I have always addmired you. You were the one who set me on the path of success. Without you, I would be nothing. Thank you, Shade," Jacob said as he held out his hand to shake mine.

I took his hand. We turned back to the glass and continued watching the target. He seemed to be oblivious to our actions, but there was no way to be sure. We just had to be paitent and see what would happen as the night progressed. It wasn't fair to be toying with these humans' lives, but it was the only way we could find them and know for sure.

I gave the bouncer a tip as I entered, so that he would remember me. I walked in to see all the colors the club displayed the night before. I was hoping that Wolf and Shade would have luck finding their marks in the crowds. I, on the other hand, walked right into mine. He was slightly taller than me. He had dark hair, but in the lights, I couldn't make out a color. He felt menacing, which meant he had been around awhile. I gave me a go-to-hell look, when I bumped into him. I slide by him and kept walking.

I went to the bar to get a drink before going out onto the dance floor. This was my way of looking normal, but there was no knowing if he could sense my presence. I had to play this one on the safe side and keep my distance. I downed my drink, nodded to the bartender, and went to the dance floor. I danced for almost an hour, keeping a occasional eye on my mark. He rarely talked to anyone, but when he did, it looked like he was trying to convince them to take something. Was he druging his prey? I didn't know, but I had to find out soon. Luckily, no one seemed to want anything he was offering, so he had to keep moving.

I went back to the bar for my second drink. This time I took to shots. The bar tender gave me a curious look. I smiled and shrugged as I turned to go back to the dance floor. It was four hours before my mark had a bite. After the guy took the drug, my mark went across the room and watched him, waiting for the effects to kick in. I had to let him take this one, so I wouldn't ruin the plan, but I aimed to save the next one, even if they were victims of their own mistakes.

It took almost an hour for the drug to take effect, which lead me to believe that my mark was patient. He would prove to be very dangerous. I couldn't slip up or let one of the others slip up around him. If we did, we could all be dead by dawn. I watched as my mark walked over to the guy and offered him a ride home. Not knowing what was going on, he just nodded to what ever my mark said. The drug seemed to make the taker lose most of their senses. It made me wonder if it was designed to work on us, but I doubted such a low dose would work. I went back to the bar for one last drink, before calling it a night.

As I walked out the door, I caught a glimpse of a manhole being pulled back into place from below. This confirmed one theory we had, but still left alot to think about. I turned around to see Wolf walking up to me. He seemed happy, which meant he got his mark or had too much fun for one night. After I looked him over, I decided it was the later of the two. I put my arm around his shoulder, and pulled him back to the base. He seemed happy to follow my lead.

I got home just as the sun began to rise, I assumed. I couldn't see it yet. Even though Jacob's club stopped serving alcohol at two, they kept the party going until six. I stayed for two reasons. The first was that I had alot to catch up with Jacob. He did miss ten years of my very interesting life. The other, was that my target was still there until after five. Once again, he left empty handed, but something wasn't right. He talked to way too many people to have simply left empty handed like that. I had to find out what he was saying to those people.I openned the door to find Wolf and Cain had already returned, which was no surprise. They did seem surprised by my late arrivail. Wolf seemed to be happier than ussual, while Cain seemed more annoyed than ussual.

"What did I miss?" I asked as I set my coat down.

"Wolf's mark was a no-show," Cain growled. Wolf simply shrugged his shoulders and smiled. I got the feeling that Wolf had a secret that he didn't want us knowing.

"How was your target?" I inquired.

"Crafty. He uses drugs to subdue his prey. And yours?" Cain returned.

"He keeps leaving empty handed. I don't know if he is setting up meetings outside of the club, or if he is aware of us. Either way, he is smarter than I gave him credit. Seems like they all are," I deduced.

"No arguements here," Wolf addmitted. This told me that he was definately hiding something from us. With the way Cain looked at him, I could only assume that Cain felt the same way.

"We will have the meeting I an hour or two. That gives us some time to relax and unwind," Cain decided.

FOLLOWING THE TRAIL

CAIN WAS GETTING READY FOR THE MEETING, while Wolf was in the shower. I decided that this was my best chance to see what Cain thought about Wolf's behavior. I'm sure he would agree that it was suspicous. I walked over and sat down. Cain looked up from what he was doing and sat down opposite of me.

"You want to discuss Wolf, don't you?" Cain guessed.

"You guessed it," I said with a nod.

"Well, what do you think?" Cain inquired.

"I think he's hiding something that happened last night. I severly doubt he's a spy, but something happened that he doesn't want us to know. Do you have anything to add?" I explained.

"Only that I believe it isn't any of our business, because I think I know what it is, but I need more information before being certain. Is that fair to you?" Cain added.

"Very much so," I said.

The shower turned off. Cain and I decided that our conversation was over. We sat there patiently waiting for Wolf to join us. When Wolf finally joined us, it was six in the evening. He sat down next to me and looked at Cain, waiting for him to start the meeting.

"Now that Wolf has joined us, we can begin. Tonight we need to try and follow them. If you think they know what you are, stay out of their way. We don't want any unnessasary conflicts. It may cost us more than we can afford to give. Any questions?" Cain decided.

"What if they don't show?" Wolf asked.

"If your mark doesn't show, go down the manhole down the street from my spot. I want you to explore them without being caught," Cain answered.

"I shouldn't have any problem following my target. How far do we go?" I asked.

"Until you feel others. It would be too risky any other way," Cain declared.

"And if it's a trap?" Wolf inquired.

"Do your best to escape with your life," Cain said with a deadly serious look on his face. It looked as though he expected at least one of us to run into trouble.

Wolf and I both nodded to acknowledge what Cain had just said. Cain stood up and put his jacket on. Wolf and I both looked at each, unsure of what Cain was doing. It was much too early to go to the clubs. Cain walked to the door and openned it. Wolf and I both stood up to join him, but he just smiled at us as he walked out the door. Wolf and I just looked at each other with utter amazement.

"Where do you think he?" Wolf began.

"Sightseeing?" I suggested.

"We'll go with that," Wolf decided. I just nodded.

"Um.... I don't know what to do," Wolf addmitted.

"Ya know what?" I said with a grin.

"No I don't," Wolf said with a confused look on his face.

"I'm gonna go out and explore the city," I declared.

"That sounds like a plan," Wolf agreed.

"Then it's settled. See you in a few hours," I told Wolf as I headed for the door.

"Wait, what about me?" Wolf demanded.

"Have fun," I said with a smile as I walked out the door.

I walked down the street for a few minutes before realizing that Cain was too far away to have gone by a cab. I blurred to an alley near the Empire State building. I made sure the coast was clear before climbing the side of the closest building and jumping the rest of the way up the skyscraper. The veiw was one of the best I had ever seen. I stood there for a moment, but decicded it was best not to stay very long. I jumped to the next building, rolling as I hit the roof. I blurred away to check on Wolf. By the time I was done with that, it would be time to get to the clubs.

I found Wolf getting a slice of pizza. It was bigger than any pizza I would find in alabama, but not enough to fill one of us. Wolf was half way done with it by the time I got to him. He didn't even look up as I approached. He just kept consuming the pizza and ignored me. Cain was a few minutes behind me. He seemed just as interested in the pizza as Wolf was. I took a seat and waited for Wolf to finish. Wolf had two bites left when Cain ripped it from him and finished it. I stood up and looked at them both.

"We ready?" I asked.

Wolf and Cain both nodded with saticfied smiles on their faces. We blurred over most of the way to the clubs. We decided to walk the last couple of blocks to prevent suspicion. We each went our seperate ways so we weren't linked to each other. It was a sound plan so far, so we decided to stick with it.

I made it to Jacob's club as the bouncer stepped out of the door to start letting people in. He let me in first. I went straight to Jacob's office. He was standing there unlocking it. He smiled when he saw me and held the door open for me. We walked in and shut the door. Jacob went to his desk, while I took a seat by the window. He used his intercom to order us some drinks. We watched as the club filled with people. My target showed up when the club was about half full. I watched his every move looking for a way to predict when he would pick his prey and leave. Nothing he did made alot of sense making it very hard to be able to figure him out.

I watched as he moved through the crowd talking to almost everyone he came into contact with. Jacob didn't seem as talkative as he had been the last couple of nights, but I was okay with that. He did, however, seem to be watching me more than my target. I was begining to think he was up to something. I would have to watch him from now on.

I made it to the club and went straight to the dance floor. I was sure that Wolf and Shade had made it to their spots by now. I spotted my mark on the other side of the dance floor. This was my que to get a drink. I slipped through the bar and ordered a drink. The bartender nodded. My mark had a simuliar idea. He walked right next to me and ordered a beer. He grabbed the bottle, nodded to me, and walked around the edge of the dance floor.

I downed my drink and ordered another. Someone in the corner waved to my mark. He walked over to them. After a minute of talking, my mark slide something into the person's hand. My mark walked away, but not too far. I downed my second drink and returned to the dance floor. I didn't pay my mark any attention for about half an hour. When

I checked on him and his prey, the drug was starting to take effect. My mark made his move, which meant it was time for my to make mine.

I followed my mark as he lead his prey out the front door. I nodded to the bouncer as I stepped out. He just nodded behind me as if he knew what I was after. I glanced over my shoulder to see my prey turning a corner. I nodded to the bouncer again before turning to go after my mark. I stopped at the corner for a split second, then walked into the alley. I saw a manhole slide back into place. I walked over to it and knelt down. I sensed that my mark was moving away form me fast. I quickly moved the manhole and started climbing down. I replaced the manhole before continuing to follow my mark. I blurred down each part stopping to check on his progress. He finally stopped moving after we had made it across town. I looked around the corner to see what I could. My mark slide into a hole in the side of the sewer. There was a guard standing next to it. I jumped across the sewer and knelt down on the other side to watch wait was going on. I knew the others would be along before the night was out, and I planned on getting out of here with them. After that, we could get in touch with the others and let them know what we found, just in case.

I sensed someone coming, but one of them was Wolf. I thought that he was following his mark at first, but he was too close to be following. He blurred next to me with his mark at his side. She stayed close to him almost as if she were his mate. It made sense now. He linked with her. That's why he said she wasn't there the night before and then behaved suspiciously. He was her match. They were made for each other, and she seemed to have joined us. I raised an eyebrow, and Wolf nodded. They both took a knee next to me to wait for Shade and his target. With her on our side, we didn't need to tail them anymore, but I could understand why Wolf was hiding it from us. He wanted to be sure that we would trust him and not kill her.

I continued to watch my target as Jacob ordered us another drink. Finally, for the first time since I laid my eyes on him, my target made his move. He talked a girl into leaving with him. I turned to Jacob and nodded in farwell. He looked aggrivated, but quickly composed himself and nodded back. I rushed out of his office and down the stairs. I went out the front door and saw the target making his why down the street with the girl. I walked into the closest alley and jumped onto the roof. I followed them from up there. My target didn't seem to notice me as he walked with the girl. They turned down an alley close to where Cain was positioned. My target whispered something in the girl's ear and she went limp. My target openned a manhole and climbed down. Oddly, he left it open as if he knew someone else was going to be useing it.

I jumped off the roof after I gave him some time to get some distance. He wasn't blurring like I thought he would be. I waited another minute, before jumping down after him. I landed with a splash. Standing right infront of me was my target. Another guy was taking the girl away. I was found out, and it looked as though they planned on killing me right now. I stood there waiting for him to make his move, but he didn't do anything. I tilted my head with curiosity. A smile appeared on my target's face. It was a long minute before anything happened.

"Very clever. So how many of you are there exactly?" my target asked.

"More than enough," I answered refusing to help this guy.

"My name is Mark. I killed on of you guys a few days ago. He was desent in the fight, but not anywhere near strong enough to even harm me," Mark introduced himself.

"I'm not sure if that is a warning, a threat, or an implication, but trust me when I say, you are about to die," I informed my opponent.

"You aren't like us. We are trained for war. We will prevail," Mark stated as he drew a dagger.

Before Mark could even take a step toward me I sent a wave of power at him. He was sent flying into the wall of the sewer. He landed on his knees, dropping his dagger. He slowly stood up clenching his fist. He blurred toward me with more speed than anyone I had ever seen. I put up a shield just before he got to me. He smashed into it. The force shattered my shield sending both of us flying several feet. I landed on my feet and charged him. Mark landed on his head and bounced onto his knees. He looked up just in time to see me ram him. He slide back several feet. A silver gleam caught my eye just behind him, so I sent another wave of power at him with one open spot. The wave sent him back into the wall. I ran up and caught his dagger as he recovered and charged. I focused a wave around my arm and put a shield. He ran into my shield, breaking it, but this time it didn't stop him. I threw my arm up stopping him dead in his tracks. I thrusted his dagger up, stabbing it up his jaw, into his brain. I grabbed his head with the same arm and ripped it off. I threw his head down the sewer. I slammed my arm into the sewer wall to set the bones back. I knew he would most likely break the bones in my arm if I used it to stop him, but it was the best solution. Once I had reset every bone I could I rushed to find the one who got away. If I could find him, I would be able to meet back up with the others, who were most likely waiting for me.

WOLF'S STAND

Cain and I were waiting for Shade to get here so we could take Lisa back to the others to get the information we needed. It was sure to be dawn soon so I hoped that Shade was on his way. I had a very uncomfortable feeling, that I just couldn't figure out. I turned to look at Lisa, she looked very worried about something. She hugged my waist as something got our attention. There were two figures coming down the sewer. One was carrying the other. I could sense Shade now and he was still a good ways behind this guy. The figure turned down a passage a few feet infront of us. Shade rounded the corner at the other end of the sewer and started our way. Cain blurred to the other side of the passage to stop Shade from following them any further. Lisa and I blurred over to them once Shade had come to a stop.

"We have to leave now. Wolf's mate, Lisa can give us all the information we need," Cain explained to Shade.

"We will have to come back though. I have to avenge Echo's death," I interjected.

"The one who did it is dead," Shade stated calmly. It was then that I realized that his left arm looked messed up.

"Then we will be done with this mission once we get out of here," Cain established.

"But you won't get out of here alive," a voice echoed from behind us.

We turned to see six figures standing a few feet behind us. Two of them were slender women, one with dark hair, the other with blonde. Of the four men, two were small, one was about average, while the other was big all around. All four of the men had dark hair. They were blocking us from going that direction, not that we needed to.

"We're surrounded," Shade said from behind me. I looked over my shoulder to see three more figures standing in our way. Two of them were girls with dark hair. The guy was kind of small with blonde hair. They didn't seem like much, but when it comes to our kind, you never know what to expect. At least one of us had to make it out. Shade and Cain had both proven to be important generals in this war, so they were the ones who had to survive. I hoped that Lisa would understand why we had to part ways so soon. I took a step away from the others. I launched myself at the three that were blocking our most likely escape route. I slammed into them creating a large gap for the others.

"Go, I'll hold them off so you three can escape!" I yelled. Shade and Cain were already on the other side of me. Lisa was standing between me and the other six. "Lisa, run!"

"I won't leave the man I love to die alone," Lisa said as the other began walking toward her.

"We won't leave you either," Shade said as he stomped his foot down onto one of the downed opponents. He crushed the girl's chest and kicked her head off.

"We will all leave here together," Cain added as he crushed the guy's head.

We all realized it all at once, there were over a hundred other Forsaken close by, and they were getting closer. I took out my hunting knife, and slit the other girl's throat, before stabbing her in the chest. I stood up and blurred to Lisa's side. It was too late for all of us to out run these six. It was pointless to fight them together,even if we could kill them all. By the time we were done, the large mass of Forsaken headed toward us, would be here, and we would all be dead. Someone was going to have to stay and it had to be me.

"You guys go on. It's too late for all of us to get out of here," I called back.

"Never," Cain shouted.

"We don't leave out own behind," Shade insisted.

"I'm going to die with you," Lisa stated.

"Cain, Shade, you two have to live to tell the others. Lisa and I will leave a dent in these guys, now go or this will be for nothing," I explained. I knew they would go, because they had to, end of story.

"Give em hell," Cain ordered as he turned and blurred out of sight.

"We will remember this," Shade said as he turned to blur away.

Two of the six went to blur around us, but I stopped one of them before he could get by me. The other four went for the gap between Lisa and me. I kicked off the wall and stopped all but one. Lisa had hold of the other one who tried first. She swung him into the wall causing it to start falling around us. This worked to my advantage, I pushed two of them into the falling debris. I threw my leg back, kicking on of the others in the chest. She went flying into the wall. The other girl rammed me, but I rolled, throwing her down the sewer passage. Lisa grabbed a pipe and rammed it through one of the other's chest. He dropped as she was grabbe by one of the other two. I threw my knife into that one's head, giving Lisa a chance to get free. I knocked the other one I threw into the falling debris, into the wall and ran to Lisa's side. I grabbed a peice on debris and smashed the skull of the one who had my knife in his head.

That left the two girls and just one guy. The mass of Forsaken were almost here. Lisa and I were running out of time, but at least we were together. I picked up my knife and waited to see what these three were going to do. The debris made it difficult to move around, but it could be used as an advantage for me. Lisa crouched down next to me. I didn't know what she had planned, but it didn't seem like the other three did either. One of the girls leapt into the air. I prepared for her to connect, but Lisa launched a peice of debris that went straight through the girl's chest. She fell to the ground and went limp. The guy jumped up and bounced off the wall. I intercepted him and smashed his head into the wall. Before he could free himself, I stepped on his back and pushed down. His head rolled out of the wall as his body hit the ground. I turned to see Lisa take a blow to the side of her head. The last girl was limping and couldn't use her left arm. I spun her around and lifted her onto my shoulder. I swung her head into the wall, crushing it.

"Are you okay?" I asked Lisa.

"Is that a trick question?" Lisa laughed.

"You know it isn't," I told her. The mass of Forsaken were almost on top of us.

"I know," Lisa said as she put her hand on my face.

I kissed her hand and helped her up. We turned toward the sound of a hundred footsteps coming closer. I turned to face her. Lisa looked happy, even though we were about to die, she looked undeniably happy. I pulled her toward me and kissed her for the first time since I set eyes on her. She wrapped her arms around me as she embraced the kiss. I pulled back and looked at her. She had a determined look on her face.

"What are you thinking?" I had to ask.

"Let's at least try to survive," Lisa said.

I nodded and we blurred away as fast as we could. It was a maze down here, but we just tried to put as much distance between us and the mass as we could. I lost track of the turns we took, but we were lost. We came to a dead stop after a few minutes of blurring. I looked around, but there was nowhere to run.

"It's a dead end," Lisa confirmed.

"Now what?" I asked myself.

"I don't know," Lisa said as she hugged me. We could hear footsteps getting closer.

"I guess we will have to fight to the death anyway. At least, I found you," I told her as I kissed her one last time.

The footsteps were almost on us. We turned and prepared to face impossible odds, together. I took one last look at Lisa before the mass would be upon us.

WHAT TO DO NOW

WE DIDN'T KNOW WHAT WOULD BECOME OF Wolf, but we knew that when this was all over, he would be known as a hero. I stopped and turned. Cain did the same, but he looked confused, until our persuer was in sight. I backhanded him when he was within my reach. He slammed into the wall. Cain was already there to finish him. Cain ripped his spine out and threw it down.

Cain turned to blur away again, but I stopped him. He gave me confused look as he turned to face me. I smiled and pointed up. There was a manhole right above us. Cain went up first to see if it was safe. He motioned for me to follow him. I jumped out. He closed the manhole behind me. We blurred back to the main part of the city to get a cab. We got back to the office as the sun was coming up. My phone started vibrating. It was Rose so I answered quickly.

"Hey beautiful, I just got home. How are things?" I answered.

Rose told me about things that were going on in the house and around town. It seems that the town called an investigation on my house. Of course, they found nothing, but a bunch of guys. I made the phone call as quick as possible, because the quicker I got things taken care of here, the quicker I got back to Rose. Cain was in the shower the whole time, but he finished as I was getting off. He helped me reset all of the bones I couldn't do myself so my arm would work right again. Then, I jumped in the shower. When I got out, Cain was sitting there waiting for me.

"He didn't make it did he?" I asked as I took a seat.

"He died a hero. I just got off the phone with Mathew. He has assembled most of the Forsaken at his place. They will be here in a few hours, probably in the morning. We need to just lay low until then," Cain explained.

"Something is bothering me. My target knew when I was there, and when I was making my move. I was set up," I thought outloud.

"Who could have possibly betrayed you without betraying us?" Cain wondered outloud.

"Jack wasn't the only one who discovered what I was. His friend, Jacob, did too. He didn't show the same lust for power so I showed him how to be successful," I told Cain.

"Do you think that he simply had more control?" Cain asked.

"I know Jacob betrayed me. The only reason that guy, Mark, did any damage to me, was cause Jacob slipped something into my drink, which means he can find us. He has the resources," I realized.

"This city just became a battlefield," Cain whispered as he realized what we had gotten into.

"We don't have until morning to stay alive. I some how doubt they will wait until dark to come after us," I announced.

It was right then that we realized we had already been found. We were surrounded and there were alot of people nearby, but I don't think that the Avengers cared anymore. They were here to kill us at all costs, and we were already at a disadvantage. I ran into the backroom and grabbed an insurance policy that I cooked up the day we got here. It was a bomb with enough force to destroy this building. Cain got the escape route ready while I set it up. The enemy was coming in for the kill. I set it for thirty seconds and ran for the exit. Cain and I were in the sewers again. We blurred away just before the blast went off. I knew the blast had killed some of the enemy, but there was no telling how many.

We found a manhole about six blocks over and climbed out of the sewer. There were a few people there to witness us getting out of the sewer, but we just ignored them. A few of the enemy had already discovered us and raced to intercept us. Cain and I both ran into an alley and jumped onto a building. We started jumping from building to building in an attempt to get away, but it wasn't working. Cain and I both stopped on the roof of a building and turned to face our persuers. There were five of them. They landed in a pentagram around us. Cain and I both smiled as we blurred into combat. I wraped myself around one of the five and riped him apart. One of the others came at me from my right side. I caught their arm, side-stepped, and riped her arm off. I spun around and knocked her over to the next building with her own arm. A third came at me from my now front side. I slapped him with the arm I was still holding and then put my hand through his chest. I blurred over to the girl and riped her arm in half and stabbed her with each half, one through the neck and the other through the heart. Cain blurred next to me.

We were both covered in blood. We went back to jumping from building to building. This time we had a destination. We were going to Jacob's club to make him talk. It was only a few more blocks, but the area was starting to look full of people. It looked as though the cops were there. They were putting some of the bouncers we saw into the back of their cars. I spotted Jacob. He looked up suddenly and looked right at us. He knew we were here. As soon as the cops let him leave, Jacob went right into his club. Cain and I jumped to one of the buildings behind his club, but Jacob walked out the back door and jumped up to the roof to meet us.

"This is what happens when you don't share the wealth," Jacob said mockingly.

"You didn't seem to want it," I returned.

"Oh I wanted it. Unlike Jack, who couldn't control himself, I was patient, and now look at me. I'm one of you," Jacob mocked.

"You aren't even close," Cain snapped.

"How do you figure?" Jacob asked.

"Cause you don't have what it takes to kill someone like us," Cain pointed out.

"Who me? I'm here to stall you," Jacob admitted.

"You're just a pawn. We are generals. Looks like you amounted to nothing compared to me after all," I said with a sneer.

"How dare you!" Jacob snapped.

I sent a wave of power that knocked Jacob off of the roof. I blurred to the ground below and knocked him into a wall before he even hit the ground. Before he hit the ground after hitting the wall I grabbed him and slammed him into the wall. I grabbed the dumpster and slammed it down on top of him, crushing him. Blood pooled around the dumpster as I jumped back to the roof.

"You just killed our lead," Cain pointed out.

"Our lead is where we were this morning, before the sun came up," I replied.

"The sewer," Cain breathed.

"Yes, that is where we will find a way to subdue most of these guys, if not all of them," I stated.

"Okay, let's go," Cain decided.

We jumped over a few blocks. We found the spot we came out of this morning. We jumped down and quickly entered the sewer. We blurred down the tunnels until we found a section that looked as though it had been hit by a truck. This was where we were. A fight among our own would leave this kind of damage. We walked down the passage and turned down the one we watched to others go down. The guard turned to us and charged. Cain blurred ahead of me and took the guard's head off. I walked past the headless body and turned into the hole. Cain was right behind me. It was a cave the lead down. We followed to path until we saw some light. We stopped and looked inside to see what was going on.

It was a large chamber. By my count, there were eighty-two Forsaken in there. There was no way Cain and I would be able to kill them all. We needed a plan. There was one sitting on what looked to be a throne on the other side of the chamber form where we were. He had to be the leader of the Avengers, Trinity. I could end this if I could kill him. I looked at Cain and nodded. He nodded in return and followed my lead. We stepped out and walked into the great chamber.

SHOWDOWN

"Y OU DARE COME HERE, FORSAKEN," TRINITY CALLED. The others stood up, but Trinity held up his hand for them to stand down.

"I come here to challenge you so that we can end this," I announced. Cain looked bewildered. This was not what he was expecting.

"And if I refuse?" Trinity challenged.

"We will kill at least twenty of you. Then in a matter of hours, you will all be dead," I said calmly.

"You're bluffing," Trinity declared.

"Just the two of us have already killed nine of you guys. What makes you think we are lying?" I stated.

"You haven't had enough time to rally your troops," Trinity insisted.

"What makes you think that?" I inquired.

"You didn't discover us until last night. And we ambushed your place within two hours. There is no way you had enough time to get your troops ready," Trinity said full of confideince.

"They were already ready and waiting for the word. We just wanted an exact location, which we found last night. Only one of the others needs to know where you are for the plan to work. You did force us to come here though. With several of your men on the street this was the best place to go. And by challenging you, we give ourselves a chance to survive this onslaught," I explained.

"You are either a very good liar, or you are telling the truth. As much as I want you dead now, I think it would be best to save my men, considering I know how many you and your friend have killed already. I accept your challenge, but only one of you will fight me. Decide amongst yourselves who my opponent will be," Trinity decided.

"I'll handle the fighting," Cain said without hesitation.

"No Cain. We need to decide who is best suited for this fight and who would be able to take out the most in the case of a loss," I tried.

"Shade, he is the oldest of them, and I am the oldest of us," Cain began.

"Only cause I killed Lilith," I interupted.

"True, but I have been the leader for a long time now. This is a leader on leader fight. It is my responsibility," Cain stated.

"I'm the leader too," I interjected.

"Second in command," Cain insisted.

"You said I was your equal," I corrected.

"Will you two hurry up," Trinity demanded.

"Shade, just let me fight," Cain insisted.

"No, this was my idea," I said as I shook my head.

"Enough! The one who issued the challenge will be my opponent since the two of you can't make up your minds," Trinity decided.

I nodded while Cain cursed under his breath. I stepped forward and Trinity stood up. He leapt from his balcony overlooking the chamber and landed a few yards infront of me. He removed his cloak to reveal and older man wearing several swords. This explained why most of the Avengers used blades. He waved to one of his followers. The follower threw two swords at my feet. I pulled them from their sheathes to reveal one-sided blades, katanas. Trinity drew two of his swords. They looked to be long swords.

"You seem to be aquainted with several types of swords," I pointed out.

"Yes and?" Trinity returned.

"So you're the one who taught Relic how to use a sword then?" I inquired.

"How do you know Relic?" Trinity demanded.

"I killed him," I stated without remorse.

"He was my best soldier," Trinity snapped as his temper flared.

"He was a great warrior," I stated calmly.

"You will join him soon enough!" Trinity roared.

With that said Trinity charged me. I stepped to the side, but Trinity swung his long swords to the side, forcing me to block anyway. The power he put behind his swing threw me back several feet, but I managed to keep my balance. He charged me again, this time crossing his arms with his swords at the ready. I stepped forward as he started to swing them and caught his swords as they began to cross. I tried holding my ground, but he was too powerful. I swung the sword in my left hand, forcing him to take a step back, giving me room to breath. I leapt back a few feet and waited to see what his next move was.

Unsurprisingly, Trinity charged me again. This time he dragged the sword in his left hand while pulling the other across his chest. I knew what he was going to do. He was going to swing both of them at two different heights, leaving me one way out, stepping back. If he quick stepped after that, he could thrust both swords at me. It would be next to impossible to dodge the second part of that attack, unless you knew it was coming.

Trinity did exactly as I thought he would. I stepped back and readied the sword in my left hand. As he made the second part of his attack, I stepped to the side, using the sword in my left hand to push his swords away as I jabbed the other sword into his side. Then he did something unexpected that caused him more damage and almost killed me. He used the force of my push to swing his swords up and then bring them down on my head. The twisting he did to do this made my sword slice through his side, but if I had been a second slower to jump and roll out of the way, he would have killed me. Thankfully, he only cut a gash down my chest, which hurt like hell.

Trinity threw his two long swords up and drew two of the other swords. These were katanas like mine. He threw them into the air as well and drew his last two swords. These two were wide, but not very long. The other four swords never hit the ground. They hovered next to Trinity as he stood there smiling at me.

"What's so funny?" I asked, calling his bluff.

"I have control over my swords, even when they aren't in my hands," Trinity answered with glee.

"You do realize that most of our kind develope powers like that, right?" I pointed out.

"But no one I have ever faced, has been able to stand up to my attacks for very long," Trinity tried starting to lose his confidence.

"You made this tricky, I'll admit, but not impossible," I stated calmly, throwing his calm to the wolves.

"That can't be!" Trinity exclaimed.

With that said, Trinity launched his swords at me. One swung behind me. The two katanas came in from either side. The other long sword came at me from above. Cain seemed slightly on edge, probably because he would have no trouble taking out Trinity. I took a breath and released a wave of power from my whole body, sending all of the swords flying back. Trinity didn't let up as he sent them right back at me, hoping to catch me off guard. It didn't work because I made the wave of power spiral around me and held it. Trinity's swords kept bouncing off of my spiral wave of power as he kept up his attack. I knew my aura wouldn't be able to kept this up forever, but it was my best defense.

I had to take offense, so I started shooting waves of power at Trinity. He didn't notice the first one, which caught him full in the chest sending him flying back, but he quickly recovered and saw through my attack. He started dodging which slowed his attacks, but didn't stop them. For the moment we were at a dead heat, but it wouldn't last long with my depleating aura. Oddly, I noticed that Trinity wasn't using any of his aura so he had plenty to spare. If I could get closer, I could finish this.

I slowly started walking toward Trinity, which was difficult with his constant movements. Finally, my aura was too weak to hold the spiral, so I had to start moving quicker. I started dodging his swords, which qued him into the fact that I was starting to run out of energy. He wasn't the only one. Cain took a step forward as if he was going to interfer, but several of Trinity's followers stood up to meet his challenge. I narrowly dodged another swing of his flying swords, and rolled close enough to him. I latched onto his aura with my own and started drawing it in. I rolled away from another attack, trying not to get too far away as I tried to get as much from him as I could.

I was finished when one of Trinity's attacks hit it's mark. One of the katanas went through my gut. It stunned me, giving the other katana enough time to peirce my right shoulder. I dropped to my knees just as one of the long swords would have taken my head off. Anger boiled inside me. I dropped the swords in my hands, but they never hit the ground. My aura flared sending them straight at Trinity. He was caught off guard by the sudden burst of strength so both swords peirced his chest. The two longs swords dropped out of the air a few feet away from me. Trinity stared at me in disbelief as I stood back up. I sent one last wave of power, containing everything I had left, at Trinity. His body began desintagrating as the power washed over him. I slowly pulled the two swords out as Trinity's body turned to dust. I dropped both swords, before collapsing.

Cain was at my side with his shield up, before any of the Avengers could make a move. Three or four attempted to kill us, but they just bounced off of Cain's shield. I don't know what Cain was planning, but it was unnessasary. Just as more of the Avengers were going to take a crack at Cain's shield, Mathew and about a dozen other Forsaken rushed into the chamber. The Avengers scattered in an attempt to escape, but more Fosaken poured into the chamber. I wasn't sure if they had taken care of the ones that were on the hunt, but this bunch was good enough for right now. Cain lowered his shield and knelt next to me.

"We did it, just the two of us, though I have to addmit, if Mathew hadn't showed up when he did, we might have died today. Rose would kill me if I let you die on her," Cain said with happy sound to his voice. I slowly faded out due to blood loss.

WHERE I BELONG

I CAME TO AFTER A FEW MINUTES. My wounds had healed, and my lost blood was being refilled slowly, but surely. I can honestly say that I was happy to be back in this small town. I would be able to relax with Rose for as long as life would allow. Some of the Avengers did manage to escape, but Skull had a team out looking for them. We were confident that a dozen of us would be able to subdue any number of them we might encounter. My biggest fear was seeing Rose. There was no telling what she had been told about what happened in New York.

I agreed to let Cain drive on the way back to the house, because I wanted no excuses to keep me form Rose. It was time that we got to live as a married couple should. I planned on living with her as if we were both humans. Cain already arranged to keep me out of the loop until Rose and I had been alone for a decade of so. I knew Rose would be happy to know that all I did gave us the time we wanted so badly. We pulled into my drive way to find Rose and Steven standing there waiting on us. I didn't even wait for the car to stop before jumping out to have her in my arms.

We met in the middle and embraced each other. I kissed her like it was the first time ever. I lifted her into the air to hold the moment as Cain parked my car. Steven walked over to Cain and shook his hand. I set Rose down and looked into her eyes. I saw the happiness that I had been longing my whole existance. I waved my farwell to Cain, without looking, and lifted Rose into my arms. I carried her into the house and shut the door behind us. This was where I belonged all along.